"You've made it quite plain that you aren't trying to marry me."

Danielle saw red. "And I never was, no matter what you thought. It wasn't my idea that inheriting a house together would propel us toward matrimony."

"So why shouldn't we enjoy ourselves?" Deke asked. "We're a great combination—now that you understand there's nothing permanent about it."

"I not only understand that, Deke, I'm glad of it."

"Then what's the big deal? We had fun together, and we could again." He reached for her hand....

Leigh Michaels has always loved happy endings. Even when she was a child, if a book's conclusion didn't please her, she'd make up her own. And though she always wanted to write fiction, she very sensibly planned to earn her living as a newspaper reporter. That career didn't work out, however, and she found herself writing for Harlequin instead—in the kind of happy ending only a romance novelist could dream up!

Leigh loves to hear from readers; you can write to her at P.O. Box 935, Ottumwa, Iowa, 52501-0935 U.S.A.

Look out for *The Boss and the Baby* by Leigh Michaels in May, in our fabulous MARRYING THE BOSS miniseries.

Books by Leigh Michaels

HARLEQUIN ROMANCE®
3444—THE PERFECT DIVORCE! (50th title)
3463—BABY, YOU'RE MINE!
3478—THE FAKE FIANCÉ
3496—THE BILLIONAIRE DATE*
3500—THE PLAYBOY ASSIGNMENT*
3504—THE HUSBAND PROJECT*

* **Finding Mr Right** Trilogy

Her Husband-
To-Be
Leigh Michaels

HARLEQUIN®

TORONTO • NEW YORK • LONDON
AMSTERDAM • PARIS • SYDNEY • HAMBURG
STOCKHOLM • ATHENS • TOKYO • MILAN • MADRID
PRAGUE • WARSAW • BUDAPEST • AUCKLAND

ISBN 0-373-03541-1

HER HUSBAND-TO-BE

First North American Publication 1999.

This edition published by arrangement with Harlequin Books S.A.

® and TM are trademarks of the publisher. Trademarks indicated with
® are registered in the United States Patent and Trademark Office, the
Canadian Trade Marks Office and in other countries.

Printed in U.S.A.

CHAPTER ONE

HE DIDN'T often come to the Willows anymore, so Danielle was startled when she looked up from the maître d's stand, flashing the smile with which she greeted every customer, and saw him just inside the door. Her heart jolted as if she'd had a close encounter with a defibrillator.

With surprise, she thought. *Definitely not with pleasure.*

She had to admit, though, that Deke Oliver was as easy on the eyes as he'd ever been. Tall and straight and lean, his almost black hair as perfectly cut as his herringbone jacket, his face as perfectly chiseled as a Roman statue...

It was just too bad the man inside didn't match up with the glorious exterior. If he had—well, then Deke Oliver would really have been something.

"Hello, Danielle," he said. "A table for two, please."

His voice was like hot fudge sauce sliding over vanilla ice cream, slow and rich and sensual. Once, Danielle had thought it was the sexiest thing she'd ever heard. Now she knew it was just part of the man's stock-in-trade. In Deke's profession, a voice that invited women to swoon over him must come in handy.

With just a hint of amusement, he added, "At least I presume the restaurant's accepting business, since you're standing here?"

Danielle wondered what he'd do if she shook her head sadly and announced that since he hadn't made a reservation she really couldn't find him a table.

He'd probably barge past me into the dining room, she reflected, *and take his choice.*

"Of course we're open." Danielle smiled sweetly up at

him and admitted, "I wasn't ignoring you, Deke. It's just that I was racking my brain trying to recall which is your favorite table. You'll have to forgive me for letting it slip my mind."

The woman at Deke's side giggled a little. "Surely it hasn't been that long since you've been out for lunch, Deke."

For the first time since they'd come in, Danielle looked directly at the woman. She'd never seen so much bleached-blond hair outside of a shampoo commercial. "Hello, Norah. I'd heard you were home." Waiting out a divorce, the gossips said—but it would hardly be tactful to mention that. Danielle reached for a pair of menus and led the way into the main dining room.

The lunch rush was just getting under way, and since the restaurant wasn't yet busy, several good tables stood vacant. She hesitated for no more than a second before turning toward a secluded corner.

The table we used to share, Danielle thought. But it was also the best one available at the moment, a fact that had far more impact on her decision than unpleasant history did.

"I see it hasn't slipped far from your mind after all," Deke said gently as he held his guest's chair.

And if I'd taken him to another table, Danielle thought irritably, *he'd have no doubt said something about my wanting to protect my memories*! She didn't bother to answer, just handed each of them a menu.

Norah didn't even glance at hers, but laid it aside and leaned toward Deke. Her voice was low and throaty. "I'm sure I'll like whatever you order for yourself."

Danielle signaled a waitress and went back to the foyer. *With any luck I can stay out of hearing range*, she told herself. Which was more than she could say about Norah's perfume; there was no avoiding the scented trail she'd left.

At the register, a small redhead was counting the contents

of the cash drawer. She looked up from the stack of bills she was thumbing through and raised an eyebrow. "What are you growling about, Danny?"

"The weather."

Pam Lanning stuffed the bundle of bills into a bank bag. "But it's beautiful. The sun's shining, the breeze is warm, and if we didn't both have to work..." Her voice softened. "It's Deke Oliver again, isn't it? The office door was half-closed, but I thought I heard his voice out here."

"If I was in a bad mood—and please notice that I'm not admitting I am—it would take more than Deke Oliver to put me there. He's ancient history, Pam. It's been—what, a year now?"

"Not quite, and I'd bet that you could tell me almost to the hour if you wanted to. Besides, the reason I think he's still important to you is that there's been nobody else since."

"Of course there has. I've dated—"

"Once in a while, and no more than a couple of times each."

"Well, you have to admit the choice around Elmwood has gotten a little thin."

"Of course I admit it. Why do you think I imported Greg? Nobody's saying you should get married, Danielle."

"On the contrary. *Everyone's* saying it. You know what the gossips are like in this town." Danielle's tone was matter-of-fact. "Another year and they'll start whispering about what's wrong with me."

Pam went straight on as if she hadn't been interrupted. "But you don't even have a social life."

"Of course I do. I'm coming to your party this weekend."

"You'd enjoy it a whole lot more if you weren't coming alone."

"It's going to be such a boring party I'll need extra entertainment? *Now* you tell me."

"Stop changing the subject, Danny. Where's the harm in going out with someone for a movie now and then?"

"The harm comes when they don't want to keep it casual and you do—and you keep running into them over lunch." Danielle picked up a stack of menus and tapped them against the counter till the pile was straight and square.

"Like Deke Oliver."

"Are you back to him again? As a matter of fact, that wasn't who I meant."

"Then who? You mean Kevin hasn't given up yet?"

"Almost, I think." The front door opened, and in relief Danielle turned to greet the newcomers.

"Well, it's about time," Pam mused. "Of course, showing guys the door is getting to be a habit, Danny. You never have told me exactly why you broke up with Deke."

And I was hoping you wouldn't notice that, Danielle thought. She smiled at the Goodwins, who were among her favorite customers, and led them toward their usual table in the solarium. Half of her felt guilty for simply walking off instead of answering Pam, even though it was her job and not rudeness that took her away. The other half, Danielle admitted, felt guilty for not telling the truth about Deke. Yes, she'd been the one who'd officially called a halt to what most of Elmwood had expected would soon be an engagement, followed closely by a wedding. But in fact—

"I was really surprised to see it," Mrs. Goodwin was saying as Danielle handed her a menu. "I thought they were doing very well." She shook out her napkin and looked up expectantly at Danielle. "And with the strawberry festival coming up and everything…"

Danielle was startled. *You ought to know better than to*

let your mind wander, she scolded herself. What on earth was the woman talking about?

Mr. Goodwin said gruffly, "Always did think it was a silly idea. Begging your pardon, of course, Danielle—but Elmwood's not big enough to support a fancy hotel. The new motels are one thing, but this—"

"It's not a hotel, George. It's a bed-and-breakfast." Mrs. Goodwin tipped her head to one side like an inquisitive robin and peered up at Danielle. "You didn't know, then, that there's a Closed sign in front of the Merry Widow?"

Apprehension tingled through Danielle's veins. That was silly, she told herself. The Merry Widow wasn't her concern anymore. "Perhaps the Jablonskis are taking a little vacation."

"Right before a holiday weekend?" Mrs. Goodwin scoffed. "And leaving a sign out front telling everyone they're gone? Elmwood may be an old-fashioned town, but most folks are smart enough not to hang out an invitation to thieves nevertheless."

Danielle couldn't argue with that. "Are you certain they're gone? Maybe they just needed a couple of days' break, so they pulled the shades and took the telephone off the hook."

Mrs. Goodwin shook her head. "Didn't look that way to me. All those silly figurines she kept on the front porch are gone."

Danielle frowned. It didn't seem likely that Kate Jablonski would have moved all her ceramics if she was only going away for a few days. But it was even less likely that the Merry Widow would have closed with no notice, no rumors... *Not in Elmwood*, she reflected, *where nothing is too minor for gossip!*

Pam was zipping the bank bag when Danielle returned to the maître d's stand. "Anything you need from the bank?'' she asked. ''I noticed the register's low on ones and fives, so I'll drop those off before the dinner rush.''

Danielle shook her head. ''I can't think of anything else. Pam, would you drive past the Merry Widow on your way to the bank?''

''Sure. It's the most direct route anyway. Why?''

''Because I want to know what the new sign out front says.''

Pam looked thoughtful. ''You still aren't over your infatuation with that house, are you?''

''Of course I am. It's big and drafty and expensive and impossible—''

''And very, very romantic. If you're not still in love with it, why should you care what kind of sign the Jablonskis put up? You don't own it anymore.''

Technically, Pam was right. Danielle *didn't* own it any more—not even the half that had once, very briefly, been hers. On the other hand... ''Call it curiosity, all right? I just want to know.''

Pam dropped the bank bag and put both hands to her throat in mock horror. ''Danny, please tell me you're not turning into one of Elmwood's old gossips!''

''Of course I am. If you can't beat 'em, join 'em, my mother always said. Now that I'm past twenty-five and there's not a man in sight, what choice do I have but to start minding other people's business?'' Danielle burst into laughter. ''Pam, if you could see your face—''

''It was your tone of voice that did it. You sounded every bit as self-righteous as Mrs. Hansen when she's on a roll.'' Pam grinned. ''All right. I started it, so I've got no one to blame but myself. You can knock it off now—I've got the message that I shouldn't keep asking why you're interested in the Merry Widow.''

''Then at least we've accomplished something,'' Danielle murmured. She looked over her shoulder into the dining room to check that the large table in the center was ready, then went to greet the first of a group of businessmen coming in for their regular Thursday luncheon.

The busboy was just setting the last water glass into place as she showed the men to the table. Danielle ran an eye over the settings and gave the busboy an approving nod.

A high, tinkling laugh rang out from the corner table, and despite herself, Danielle turned to look. Norah had placed a hand on Deke's sleeve and was leaning toward him with an expression of calculated worship. Danielle wondered if the woman really thought Deke Oliver was such an inexperienced fish that he'd succumb to that lure.

And she wondered if Deke knew about the Merry Widow. He had every bit as much reason to be interested as she did. After all, he had—once upon a time—owned half of it, too.

Not that she was going to stroll over and ask, of course, or share the bit of information she had. Long training had taught her never to interrupt a customer, and in this case she'd look as if she was trying to sidetrack Deke's conference—or whatever it was—with Norah and focus his attention on herself. It was hardly the impression she wanted to make.

Besides, Danielle had far more important things to do. The lunch rush had taken hold with a vengeance; three parties were waiting when she got back to the entrance, and from then on there wasn't a chance to draw a long breath, much less think up explanations for the Jablonskis' sign.

But the question nagged at the back of her mind nonetheless. The Merry Widow had opened as a bed-and-breakfast just eight months ago, and this should be the start of the busiest season. The Memorial Day holiday that marked the traditional opening of summer was this weekend, and it would be closely followed by the end of the school year, freeing families to travel. Elmwood's strawberry festival, the most important civic event of the year, was next week.

The last time Kate Jablonski had been in the Willows she'd told Danielle that the Merry Widow's reservation book was already full for festival time. Which indicated that wherever the Jablonskis had gone, they fully intended to be back in plenty of time to cash in on those reservations. Didn't it?

The rush ended as abruptly as it had begun. Danielle made change and small talk for a few of the businessmen who'd lingered over their coffee, waved goodbye to the busboy as he clocked out for the day, and took a couple of phoned reservations for the evening hours. Only a few scattered tables were still occupied; one of them was the corner where Deke and Norah sat.

Their waitress was frantic. "I took the check to the table twenty minutes ago, but they're still just sitting there," she told Danielle. "And I can't wait any longer because I've got an appointment with my doctor. You know how hard it is—"

"To plan anything in this business. I know. Go on, Sally. I'll be here anyway."

One by one the scattered tables emptied, and eventually Deke and Norah emerged from the dining room. "I had no idea of the time," Norah was saying. She smiled up at Deke and patted his tie. "You just made me forget everything else, you charming man."

Only the self-discipline born of her years of dealing with customers kept Danielle from rolling her eyes heavenward. She focused on Deke's credit card instead, punching in the numbers and codes, wishing that he'd paid cash. Then she wouldn't have to wait even thirty seconds for the computer to issue the necessary authorization; she could just give him his change and he'd be gone.

He leaned on the counter, eyeing the book she'd pushed

aside. Danielle told herself it was silly to be sensitive about her choice of reading matter; if she wanted to read applied statistical methodology in her spare time, it was no one's business but her own. A correspondence course wasn't her first choice, but it was better than making no progress toward her degree. And someday, when her father's health was enough better that she could go back to school, she'd be happy to have statistics out of the way.

Norah peered over the cash register at the book and shuddered. "Danielle here was always the brainy one. I never could understand things like that." She slid her hand through the crook of Deke's elbow. "I'm so lucky to have found you to help me with my investments."

He signed the credit slip and pushed it back across the counter to Danielle. "I'll certainly do my best to take good care of your money, Norah."

Danielle wanted to laugh at the expression of blank surprise that flitted across Norah's face. But a split second later, the blonde had recovered and looked as if she'd never been startled in her life.

They were the last customers to leave. Danielle tucked Sally's tip into an envelope and wrote her name on it, then made a quick inspection of the dining rooms, almost entirely ready for the evening trade. She paused in the kitchen, where the cooks were already starting preparations for the dinner hour, to snatch a hard roll and a chunk of cheese, then locked the main door with a sigh of relief. In a little more than two hours, she'd have to be back, ready to take on the dinner crowd. But at least the next two hours were hers.

And there was no doubt about the first thing she wanted to do. The fact that Pam hadn't called back to the Willows to report on the Merry Widow's new sign had only increased Danielle's curiosity.

The Willows lay on the outskirts of Elmwood, in the

newer section, while the Merry Widow was only a stroll away from the restored Victorian square that had once been the main business district at the center of town. Now the square featured specialty shops and antique stores, popular draws with the sort of customer who liked staying in an elegant old Queen Anne bed-and-breakfast. The square and the house complemented each other like bagels and cream cheese; Danielle had thought so ever since the Jablonskis had first proposed the idea of a bed-and-breakfast.

Her little red car climbed an easy grade on which the Merry Widow sat as if holding her skirts up to keep from being contaminated by the surrounding commercial district. From the street, Danielle couldn't see any new signs, just the one the Jablonskis had hung from the front porch when they opened for business.

But she could also see no life around the place. No Joe Jablonski puttering around the grounds doing maintenance chores. No guests, though the usual check-in time was approaching. Of course, it was the slowest part of the week. The weekend travelers wouldn't start appearing till tomorrow, and most of the businessmen were already heading home for the holiday.

Danielle parked her car on the street and climbed the slope toward the front steps, pausing on the lawn to look up at the house towering above her. A classic Queen Anne, it displayed all the riotous imagination and Victorian excess of its kind—the architect hadn't missed a trick. There were pillared porches on three sides and balconies in the most unexpected places. Arches and finials and curlicues had been splashed across the walls with a lavish hand. Even the chimneys were fantastic; each showed off a different, intricate brick pattern. The house had not only a round shingled tower but for good measure a shorter square one with a pointed roof, topped with a weather vane in the shape of a bell-skirted lady.

That, Danielle had once been told, was the tower that had given the house its name, when the first owner had tumbled off a ladder while inspecting the unfinished work and left his wife—so the story went—not only financially secure but much happier without him. There was even a variation of the tale that said the abused wife had given the ladder a push so she could marry her lover, and that the doomed home owner had flung curses as he fell, swearing that his house would never shelter a happy marriage.

Danielle had always dismissed the whole story as a romantic froth, one of those too-clever-to-be-believed urban legends. But it was certainly true that the Merry Widow had seen its share of marital discord, broken hearts, failed engagements and early deaths....

As if any hundred-year-old house hadn't, Danielle reminded herself. This was no time to start feeling superstitious. And in any event, if the supposed curse on the Merry Widow had been what broke up her relationship with Deke, then the long-dead home owner had done her a major favor.

Not until she was actually on the porch did Danielle see the sign, and she wasted an instant wondering how on earth Mrs. Goodwin had spotted it. With binoculars, perhaps?

She forced herself to concentrate on the sign, a single sheet of paper taped to the frosted-glass panel in the front door. Compared to the neatly lettered announcement of check-in times that was posted just next to it, the sign looked crude. Each letter wavered, and the line of words had a decided downward slant.

Closed Till Further Notice.

That was no help at all, Danielle thought. Nothing about where to reach the owners in case of emergency, nothing about why they'd gone. And there was something about the slapdash presentation of the sign that worried her. They'd obviously left in a hurry. And yet...

Mrs. Goodwin had been right—Kate's ceramic figurines

were gone from the wide, gingerbread-trimmed porch that extended across the whole front of the house, around the corners and well back on the sides. All around Danielle were faint reminders of the statues that had stood there, rings against the soft gray paint where dust had collected under their edges. There must have been twenty of them— and that many figurines would not have been quickly or easily moved.

So if the Jablonskis hadn't left in a hurry, why hadn't they made arrangements for someone to look after the bed-and-breakfast? Danielle didn't think they had any family close by, but surely they had a friend who could step in for a few days....

"Not that it's any of my affair," she reminded herself. *The Merry Widow is not my problem.* Perhaps, she thought wryly, she should chart that sentence out on needlepoint canvas and turn it into a pillow, just as a reminder.

So why, since the house was not her concern, was she feeling the tingle of discomfort?

Slowly, she walked around the perimeter of the house, moving from porch to sidewalk and then to the porte coch-ere where she had always parked her car when she'd come to visit Miss Fischer. This was the door she'd always used, leading into the side hall of the house rather than the grand foyer....

A confusing mixture of emotions clutched at her heart. There was grief, of course; though it had been a year since Miss Fischer had died, Danielle still missed her fiercely. And sadness for the proud old woman who had been the last representative of one of Elmwood's founding families. A touch of guilt that Miss Fischer's well-meaning plans for the house she had so loved had come to nothing. A linger-ing trace of resentment that the woman had dumped such a burden on Danielle without even warning her of what was coming.

But incongruous as it seemed, there was a spark of gladness, too. If it hadn't been for Miss Fischer and the Merry Widow, Danielle might not have realized in time what Deke Oliver really was. She might have gone straight ahead and fallen in love with the man she'd thought him—and in the long run, that would have hurt even worse.

Yes, she was lucky that things had turned out as they had. Pam seemed to think Deke haunted Danielle's every waking moment—and in a sense she was right. He *was* always there, in the back corner of her mind, lurking. But not because she missed him. Not because she mourned for him. Not because she regretted their breakup.

It was because her judgment had been so badly off target. She'd been in real danger of tumbling headlong for Deke Oliver when Miss Fischer's quirky legacy had brought the real man to the surface, and the shock had battered her even more than the loss of her friend.

Now she was afraid that it might happen again. If she'd been so wrong about one man, what was to keep her from misjudging another?

She didn't hear the car in the driveway till it was almost under the porte cochere. The Jablonskis, back from whatever errand had taken them away? An unsuspecting guest, arriving on schedule? Since she didn't relish getting involved in either scenario, Danielle stepped quickly around the corner of the house rather than be caught standing in the driveway. She caught just a flash of a dark green car as she made her escape; the driver might have had an equally brief glimpse of her but only if he or she was looking in precisely the right place.

Her hands in her pockets, Danielle continued her circuit of the house. She was halfway around now anyway, so she might as well check the other side on her way back to her car.

She strolled around the back porch, the most utilitarian

feature of the house's exterior, and started up the side, where French doors in the dining room looked out over a slate-paved patio where Miss Fischer had served mint tea on warm summer afternoons. But when she saw the patio, tucked into a sort of nook between the dining-room wall and the end of the front porch, Danielle stopped dead in her tracks.

Scattered over the dark gray paving stones were bits of broken plaster. *Kate's figurines*, she thought as she stooped to pick up a fragment. It was the face of a shepherdess; Danielle remembered noticing that particular statue on one of the few visits she'd made to the Merry Widow after the Jablonskis had moved in.

She scuffed at the pieces with the toe of her shoe. At first she'd thought the figurines had simply been heaved from the end of the porch onto the slate below, but none of the bits was larger than her hand and most had been reduced to little more than white dust—as if they'd been pounded to pieces by a hammer. And the moss that had lain undisturbed between the stones for decades was gouged in places as if the weapon that had shattered the figurines had slipped now and then. As if it had been wielded in fury and none too carefully.

And if Kate's figurines had been smashed by a furious hand, Danielle thought numbly, what of Kate herself?

The sign on the front door had taken on a more sinister tone. "I don't like the looks of this at all," she muttered.

A deep, slow voice said from behind her, "It is rather a mess, isn't it?"

Danielle jumped and spun around to face Deke, standing on the grass at the very edge of the patio. "What are you doing here?" she gasped. *That was stupid*, she told herself. *Like you've got a right, and he doesn't*!

"Probably the same thing you are," Deke said mildly.

"Joe came by my apartment this morning to drop off a key, and—"

"Oh, it was nice of you to warn me before the gossips decided that Kate and Joe just walked out. If I'd known you were taking care of the place..." She paused. "Come to think of it, why *are* you taking care of the place? I didn't realize you and the Jablonskis were pals."

"We're not. And I didn't tell you because I didn't know it myself till half an hour ago. I was out with a client when Joe came by."

"Of course," Danielle said sweetly. "*Dear* Norah."

"So he left the key with the shopkeeper downstairs, and I didn't get the message till I came back after lunch. Joe said something about their marriage hitting the wall."

"That explains it," Danielle murmured. She bent and placed the shepherdess's face gently on the slate.

"The Merry Widow claims another set of victims? I thought you didn't believe in that nonsense." He didn't wait for an answer. "As a matter of fact, the gossips have it just about right. With a divorce pending, neither Joe nor Kate has any interest in the business. So they're simply walking away from it."

"Giving up?" Danielle was startled. "They're sacrificing the work and the money they've put into it?"

Deke nodded. "And washing their hands of the whole deal."

Danielle sighed. "Well, that's a relief."

"Oh, really? Then you can deal with the whole mess, since you're so pleased."

"I didn't mean... I was only saying it's a relief to know that I'm not going to find Kate in the basement with her head bludgeoned in. If he could do this to her figurines—"

"Who said he did?"

"Isn't it obvious?"

"Of course it's not. It's quite possible she did it herself.

At least Joe had enough sense and self-control to let somebody know what was going on. Kate seems to have just vanished into the sunset. But why are we fussing over figurines when we have plenty of important things to argue about?''

"Like what? It's not our prob..." She paused. "Oh."

Deke nodded. "I see you haven't quite forgotten the terms of the sale after all. Since we sold the Merry Widow to the Jablonskis with a private arrangement and financed it ourselves instead of making them get a mortgage from a bank—''

"You don't need to rub it in. I remember perfectly well that the contract sale was my idea."

Deke hesitated for a second as if he'd like to agree. Instead, he said coolly, "I wasn't placing blame, only stating the facts."

And my prissy Aunt Edna wears army boots, Danielle thought.

"It's beside the point that if we *had* insisted on a mortgage instead of agreeing to the contract, we'd be free and clear right now and the bank would be deciding what to do with the Merry Widow. We didn't, so here we are—stuck once more with the biggest white elephant in Elmwood."

"It's not a white elephant," Danielle said automatically. "Just because it's big and awkward and impractical and not in the best part of town these days doesn't mean—''

"How else would you define 'white elephant', Danielle? But since you're convinced of its value, I'll tell you what— my share's for sale, and I'll give you a great price. But no more contract arrangements. It's cash on the barrelhead this time."

"You expect me to buy you out? Not likely. I don't want this place any more than you do—and we all know what the probability is of *you* settling down and wanting a house near a school with room for a dozen kids."

"I'm glad we've at least got that much straight this time around."

Danielle gritted her teeth. She'd already said far too much. And slugging him wouldn't do any good; she'd probably break her hand against that granite jaw.

Dammit, Miss Fischer, she thought, *why did you have to go and create this mess? Why didn't you take the easy way and just leave the place to the historical society?*

She didn't realize she'd actually spoken the thought until Deke answered. "Because they didn't want it. Remember? We tried that route already."

Danielle tried to will away the evidence of her embarrassment, but her cheeks stayed hot and her tongue felt fat and useless.

Deke tipped his head back and stared up at the peak of the tower, silhouetted against the brilliant afternoon sky. "This house is like a counterfeit bill, you know. Once in your possession, it's tremendously hard to pass it on to someone else."

Danielle bridled. "Fake twenties can be shredded and thrown away. Houses can't."

Deke looked as if he'd like to argue the matter. Danielle could almost see in his mind the image of bulldozers and wrecking cranes. Then he seemed to think better of it and said levelly, "The point is that once again, we own a house. You don't want it, I don't want it—as far as I can tell, *nobody* wants it. So what in the hell do we do with it now?"

CHAPTER TWO

DANIELLE didn't know if it was the tone of Deke's voice that made her shiver or the sudden chill in the air as the spring breeze freshened. She looked up at him—at the strong line of his throat under the unbuttoned collar of his pin-striped shirt, the square-set jaw, the uncompromising mouth—then let her gaze follow his to the house.

From this angle, the Merry Widow loomed over them, looking even taller than its actual three full stories. She could almost hear the house issuing a challenge. *What are you going to do about me this time*? it seemed to be saying.

Danielle couldn't help thinking of a nightmare she'd occasionally had as a child, one that had played out the same way from start to finish each time she'd experienced it. No matter how hard she'd struggled to change the outcome, she'd been stuck; the same scary sequence of events had marched inexorably forward to the same scary conclusion.

It looked as if the Merry Widow was going to turn into precisely that kind of bad dream. Not only did they have the whole process to go through again, just as they had ten months ago, but they were just as unprepared. They hadn't anticipated the Jablonskis' defection any more than they'd foreseen the announcement that Miss Fischer's will had left her beloved house in equal shares to her young friend, Danielle Evans, and to *her* friend, Deke Oliver....

But Deke was right about one thing, Danielle reflected. He'd effortlessly put his finger on the main factor that would keep the scenario from playing out identically. This time, they knew exactly what a tough sell the house would be. Ten months ago, when they'd still been stunned by the bequest, it hadn't occurred to either of them that no one would want the Merry Widow.

It even seemed, for a while back then, that we might want it....

Knock it off, Danielle told herself. There had never been a "we". There never could have been—and though Deke's cold, blunt announcement of the fact had rasped her pride like a carpenter's file on balsa wood, at least it hadn't broken her heart. Danielle thanked heaven for being spared that particular pain.

She forced her mind back to the important question, the one she didn't want to face because it seemed unlikely the answers would come any more easily this time than they had ten months ago. What *were* they going to do about the house?

"Did the Jablonskis leave the furniture?" she asked abruptly.

"How should I know? And why should they?"

"Because it was part of the deal we made with them that the furnishings stayed with the house."

"Agreements don't always mean a lot when the pressure's on."

"You should know," Danielle said sweetly. "I don't think they could have taken out much without Elmwood noticing, though, and I haven't heard so much as a whisper. Did you say you have a key? Maybe we'd better see what we're actually dealing with."

Deke dug into his trouser pocket for a brass key. Unmarked and without even a cheerful key ring to keep it company, it looked small and lonely as it lay in his palm.

The back door swung open with a creak. "Too bad it's the wrong season for a haunted house," Deke muttered as he pushed the door wide and dropped the key back into his pocket. "This place is a natural."

Danielle ignored him and stepped over the threshold into

the kitchen. She was surprised to find that it looked almost the same as in Miss Fischer's day. Except, of course, that Miss Fischer would never have condoned the stack of dirty dishes in the sink. "I thought they were going to remodel the kitchen."

"There was a lot of talk about it," Deke mused. "But then, they seemed to have all sorts of grandiose plans—at least while they were negotiating to buy the place. It'll be interesting to see if any of them got done or if they were just talking a good game till they got possession."

"If you're implying that I was gullible in wanting them to have a chance..."

Deke's eyes narrowed. "Feeling a little sensitive, are we?"

Danielle swallowed hard.

"Anyway," Deke went on, "as far as the kitchen goes, they'd have had to install a new one before they could open a regular restaurant, as Joe said he wanted to do. But there's an exception in the law for bed-and-breakfast places—they don't have to have commercial kitchen facilities."

Danielle pushed open the swinging door into the butler's pantry and walked through to the dining room. The shades were drawn on most of the windows, and in the dim light the rooms seemed almost timeless.

The furniture had been rearranged since Miss Fischer's day; if it hadn't been for that, Danielle might almost have expected her friend to look up with a smile from the velvet slipper chair in the front parlor and lay her needlepoint aside.

But so far as Danielle could tell, nothing was missing from the public rooms. The knot in her stomach relaxed a little.

"Well, that's a relief," Deke said. "Though, on the other hand, if they'd stripped the place we'd have had a lot less to deal with." He stared at the crystal chandelier that hung at his eye level above the huge oval dining table. "You know, if we just called in an auction house—"

"Miss Fischer specified that the house and furnishings should stay together." Danielle walked on into the front foyer and stooped to pick up the envelopes scattered beneath the mail slot in the door.

"And what's she going to do about it if we don't stick to the rules? Follow us around rattling chains and shrieking down chimneys?"

"Probably only you," Danielle murmured, "since it's clearly not my idea to sell all her treasures to the highest bidder." She flipped absently through the mail, then laid it in a neat pile on the carved sideboard that served as a hall table.

"Well, I don't believe in ghosts. It's all very well to carry out the wishes of the dear departed, but sometimes what people want isn't very practical in the real world, and the ones who are left with the mess just have to do the best they can. Since we've already been down the road of selling the place as a package, with somewhat mixed results, I'm only suggesting that—"

"You know, there's a problem here." Danielle was hardly listening to him.

"Only one?" Deke leaned against the sideboard and folded his arms across his chest. "I can't wait to hear what you've singled out for special attention."

"We can't just walk in and put up a for-sale sign."

"Why on earth not? The property has reverted to us. Just as a bank can foreclose on a mortgage holder who doesn't make the payments—"

"But that's just it. The Jablonskis haven't even missed a payment yet. In fact, the next one isn't even due till…" She calculated. "Till Tuesday."

"Joe said they're walking out—leaving it all behind. A

voluntary abandonment means that we have all rights back immediately.''

"I don't doubt that you're correct about the legalities— *if* Joe really meant everything he said. But what about Kate? She's got just as many rights as Joe has, and I don't think it's terribly safe to take his word for what she thinks right now.''

Deke frowned.

"And what if they change their minds and come back?'' Danielle went on. "If they were really giving up the last hope, wouldn't they have salvaged everything they could— agreement or not? Not the furniture, maybe, that would require a moving van. But it didn't take you any time at all to spot that chandelier and know it's got some value. And it would fit in the back seat of my car, never mind the Jablonskis' van.''

Deke was shaking his head. "If you're disillusioned and sick of trying and you just want out in a hurry, you don't hang around to disassemble crystal chandeliers, no matter what they're worth. You didn't hear Joe's message.''

"But that's just it, Deke. You didn't hear it, either. I mean, you didn't talk to him yourself, so can you really judge his state of mind any better than I can?''

"Believe me—''

"What if they decide to get back together just as abruptly as they seem to have decided to split? We don't have any idea what their fight was about or how serious it really was.'' She glanced into the music room, tucked under the stairs, that the Jablonskis had turned into an office.

"Those smashed-up statues out on the patio looked pretty serious to me.''

"Oh, really? A little while ago, you seemed to think all that damage was just Kate having a temper tantrum. Which is my whole point, really. What if it was just a silly quarrel and they *do* work it out? If they come back in time to make the next regular payment and find that in the meantime we've sold the property—''

"Before Tuesday? We should be so lucky."

"You know perfectly well what I mean. We'd get hit with lawsuits from about a dozen different directions."

Deke didn't answer, but in his silence Danielle could hear reluctant agreement. Finally, he said, "A formal eviction could take months. So what do you suggest we do, Ms. Layman Lawyer? Just stand around and twiddle our thumbs while the place runs down?"

"I don't know," Danielle admitted. She reached for a leather-bound calendar that lay open on the desk and flipped the pages. Not every square was filled, but a respectable number were. And Kate hadn't been exaggerating about the list of guests already booked for the strawberry festival, little more than a week away. "It'll take days just to cancel the reservations," she muttered.

Why cancel them? asked a little voice in the back of her brain.

Danielle frowned. What kind of stupid suggestion was that? Of course they'd have to be canceled. Guests would have to be notified or they'd show up on the doorstep and be fighting mad when they found a Closed sign. And she knew better than to assume the Jablonskis had taken care of that little detail.

"I guess the trouble is," she said slowly, "that I just can't believe Kate and Joe are simply walking away from this."

"*All* this," Deke drawled. "Yes, how anyone could walk away from this treasure is certainly beyond—"

"There's no need to be sarcastic. They have a lot invested here."

"Are you certain of that? I suspect they aren't leaving behind as much as you think." Deke sat down on the corner of the desk. "The work that's been done—and there hasn't been all that much of it—Joe did himself. The grand plans to remodel the kitchen obviously came to nothing. There's a little new wallpaper and paint, but not more than a few hundred dollars' worth.''

"It's apparent,'' Danielle said dryly, "that you haven't priced wallpaper recently. But go on.''

"And though they were never late with a payment on the contract, they'd have been paying just about as much in rent if they lived somewhere else. And I have a nasty suspicion any cash that was left over didn't go back into the business.''

"Well, they had to eat.''

"Just brace yourself in case they didn't bother to pay the property taxes—because I'll make sure you get your half of the bill.''

"And what am I supposed to use to pay it?''

"How about your half of the payments the Jablonskis have been making every month?''

Danielle bit her tongue.

"Don't tell me you've been spending every cent on...'' Deke paused. "Now what *could* you have spent it all on? Not eating out, that's for sure. You must have nearly every meal at work. Or rent—you *are* still living with your dad, aren't you? Or travel. I doubt you've been out of town in the past three months. Clothes, perhaps?''

Danielle tapped her toe on the faded Oriental rug. If he dared take it upon himself to criticize her clothes, she thought grimly, she'd mop the floor with that elegant herringbone jacket of his.

Deke looked almost sad. "You really should have listened to me, Danielle, about the power of investments and compound interest. If you had, you could have been on the way to financial independence.''

"Not on half of the payment the Jablonskis were making. And what I spend my money on is none of your business.''

"Right—as long as you have enough to meet your share of the expenses. Even if we walk out right now and lock the door, there are going to be some bills along the way. We can't simply turn off the utilities, you know. And if you insist that we just let the Merry Widow sit here and gather dust till we're absolutely sure the Jablonskis aren't going to reappear..." Deke pushed his jacket back and put both hands on his hips. "How long do you think that'll be anyway? A month? Six months? Seven years, till they can be declared legally dead?"

"Don't be silly. I'm not suggesting we just let it sit here."

"Then what *are* you suggesting we do, Danielle?"

She looked down at the reservations calendar, still open to the pages set aside for the week of the strawberry festival. Then she squared her shoulders and said, "Run it."

Deke stood absolutely still, while time and Danielle's nerves stretched longer and longer. Then he threw back his head and started to laugh.

She folded her arms across her chest and waited, but her patience ran out before his hilarity diminished. "I'd love to stick around a while longer and be jeered at, but I really have things to do," she said coolly.

Deke held up a hand. "No, wait. Just give me a minute to recover. The place is already a failure, so you want to run it? And do what? Make the hemorrhage of cash even worse?"

"The Jablonskis' marriage is on the rocks," Danielle pointed out stubbornly. "That doesn't mean the Merry Widow is a failure."

"I thought you said a minute ago that they probably just had a lovers' spat."

"I said... Never mind. Whatever their problem turns out to be, it has nothing to do with the Merry Widow."

"I wouldn't be so certain of that." Deke sighed. "And

you're splitting hairs, you know. This is not exactly a record-breaking concern. If Kate and Joe couldn't make it successful, how do you expect to?''

"They had to make payments for the house."

Deke shook his head. "Oh, no. You can't disregard the value of a capital asset just because you happen not to owe a debt on it. That still has to be figured into—''

"Will you stop being a financial analyst for half a minute and just listen?''

"All right. I'm listening. What is there to gain from keeping the Merry Widow open?''

"I'd never have expected to have to explain it to you, oh great fiscal wizard,'' Danielle said crisply. "But then, most of your business experience is in the abstract, isn't it? Stocks and bonds and mutual funds and things like that?''

"And since you grew up in the restaurant trade, you know everything about running a business?''

Danielle refused to react to the irony in his voice. "Being actively involved in a retail trade is a much more practical education than an M.B.A. We've already learned that there isn't much of a market for this house—''

"This is news?''

Danielle ignored him. "As a house. But it's not just a house now, it's a business.''

"I don't anticipate that fact creating a great deal more interest. Who'd want to buy it as it stands?''

"Nobody, if it isn't running. That's the whole point.''

After a long pause, Deke nodded. "You're right.''

Danielle was annoyed. He didn't have to sound so amazed about it or act as if the admission had been forced from him. "If our best chance of selling the Merry Widow is as a bed-and-breakfast, then it has to be up and operating.''

Deke shrugged. "All right. It's true that a great deal of the value of a business is lost in the first few weeks it's closed. Of course, that's assuming that it had any value to begin with.''

Exasperated, she snapped, ''So do you have any better ideas?''

Deke leaned back into the worn velvet cushions and shook his head. ''You utterly amaze me, Danielle.''

There was a note in his voice that set Danielle's teeth on edge. If he accused her of thinking this up so she could maneuver him back into her life... Well, the sooner that possibility was wiped out of his mind, the better. She held out a hand. ''If you'll give me the key, I'll get started. Would you like regular reports or will learning about it on the grapevine be good enough?''

''Oh, I'm sure anything I need to know I'll hear about.'' There was a tiny twist of irony in his voice, and Danielle noted that he didn't waste any time digging into his pocket for the small brass key as if he couldn't wait to wash his hands of the whole problem.

And she wondered for just an instant, as she stood there holding a key still warm from his body, if she was an utter fool not to have done the same.

The rich scent of roasting prime rib wafted toward Danielle from the Willows as she got out of her car at the farthest corner of the restaurant parking lot. She'd only taken a couple of steps toward the building when Pam's car pulled in beside hers, and she leaned against a fender and waited for Pam to gather up her belongings.

''Sorry I didn't call you earlier,'' Pam said breathlessly. ''There was a crisis at school and Josh ended up at a friend's house, so I had to go retrieve him and get him to his clarinet lesson. Anyway, I didn't see any sign at the Merry Widow, and—''

''It's there. Right on the front door.''

Pam sighed. ''I might have known you couldn't stay

away. Honestly, Danny...'' Her gaze focused on the back seat of Danielle's car. ''Why is there a suitcase in your car? Your father didn't have another attack, did he?''

''No. In fact, I expect he's already here, geared up for the evening.''

''That's good. I could just see you having to go off to the hospital with him and me being stuck trying to figure out which people go with which tables. So why the suitcase? Are you eloping after work?''

''It doesn't hurt to be prepared,'' Danielle countered. ''You never know when you might meet the man of your dreams.''

''It's especially hard to anticipate the moment when you're not even looking.''

''That is a bit of a difficulty,'' Danielle admitted. She pulled open the main door and held it for Pam, who was carrying the bank bag and a box full of receipts. She was barely inside the restaurant when she spotted her father in the main dining room, moving two small tables together to accommodate a larger group, and she forgot all about Pam as she hurried to help. ''Harry, what do you think you're doing?''

''Getting ready for a party of eight,'' Harry Evans said. He leaned on one of the tables and smiled at her.

It was a half-theatrical pose that did nothing to fool Danielle. She could hear the tiny wheeze in his chest, and she wondered if his heart condition was getting worse or if he'd simply been exerting himself more than he should this afternoon. ''Dammit, Dad, you know better.'' She moved the second table into position, bracing it tightly against the one Harry was leaning on, then slid the chairs back into place. ''Let the busboys earn their pay.''

''Then why are *you* doing their work?'' Harry asked gently. He rearranged the linen napkins and place settings and strolled toward the office. ''If you have a minute,

Danielle, we need to talk about increasing our orders for next week, to be ready for the strawberry festival.''

Danielle followed. ''And making sure we have some extra help on call wouldn't hurt, either.'' Especially, she thought, since she herself was going to be wearing two hats right then—and both jobs would be demanding ones. She groaned. *I think I need my head examined.*

She straightened her shoulders. She was doing what needed to be done after all. And it wasn't as if she was taking on the Merry Widow as a lifetime commitment, just till the Jablonskis had sorted themselves out or another buyer came along. Which might not be long at all if the strawberry festival was a success.

Harry Evans dropped into his office chair with a thud, and Danielle frowned. ''I don't have to go tonight, Dad,'' she said. She'd intended to study the bed-and-breakfast's reservation book tonight and try to plan at least a few days ahead. But perhaps she could just stop by the Merry Widow, pick up the book and take it home. ''If you need me—''

Harry grinned. ''Now that's the most loaded question I've heard in a month.''

Danielle leaned against the door frame and studied him. His color had come back, and he seemed to be breathing more easily. And she knew better than to treat him like a child. The man was well past fifty, for heaven's sake.

Pam stopped sorting small bills into the cash register drawer. ''Where are you going? And does this mean I'll be shanghaied into acting as hostess for the lunch rush tomorrow? Because I warn you, Danny—''

''Of course not. I'm only going to the Merry Widow.''

''If they're closed, how can you check in for a rest cure? Besides, supporting the hometown economy is wonderful, but if I were you, I wouldn't stop within fifty miles. Too many people can find you if you stay in town.''

It wasn't as if there was any secret involved, Danielle realized. By tomorrow, all of Elmwood would know the basics; the shopkeeper who had passed on Joe Jablonski's message to Deke had no reason to keep her knowledge to herself. "I'm going to be running it for a while. Till we can sell it again."

Pam dropped a roll of quarters. The paper wrapper split and bright coins spilled across the floor. Danielle stooped to help pick them up.

"Excuse me, but is this a time warp?" Pam asked mildly. "I thought the sale was final almost a year ago."

"We thought so, too. But Joe and Kate didn't have quite a good enough credit record to get a mortgage, so we decided..." Danielle took a deep breath. "*I* decided, really, that it was worth some risk to give them a chance. So instead of making payments to a bank, they've been paying us, Deke and me, every month."

"Till now." Pam sighed. "As your accountant, Danielle—"

"Please don't start. You can't say anything Deke didn't tell me at the time."

"But he went along with it anyway?"

"I didn't give him a lot of choice," Danielle admitted. "The only other serious interest we had was from a group that was going to cut the Merry Widow up into apartments, and I couldn't stand to see that happen to Miss Fischer's house."

"So you planted your feet and fought."

Not all that hard, Danielle reflected. *But he knew I would if I had to—and by that time, Deke would have agreed to almost anything to be rid of me.* But she wasn't going to admit that to Pam; there were some wounds too tender to share even with a best friend. "After she'd trusted me with it, how could I do anything else?"

"She trusted you and Deke," Pam reminded her. "You

know, I've always wondered why she included him—why she didn't just leave the place to you. She didn't even know him, did she?''

"They met once. I went to visit her in the care center a couple of weeks before she died, and I took Deke with me.''

Funny, Danielle thought, that the whole mess really stemmed from a casual trip to the lake. They'd been on their way out of town for an afternoon's swimming when she'd remembered Miss Fischer and told Deke she'd promised to stop by to see her for a moment. And he'd come inside with her rather than wait in the June heat.

Fifteen minutes, that was all. A quarter of an hour in which he hadn't even been trying to captivate Miss Fischer—which said something about Deke Oliver's charm. He didn't *have* to try.

He'd stepped outside the room to allow Danielle a private goodbye. She hardly remembered what Miss Fischer had said, for the words had been unremarkable. Something about what a nice young man he was, a very special young man, but that obviously Danielle already knew that. And Danielle had hugged her and said, "Oh, yes. A very special man indeed.''

And from that tiny, careless comment, Miss Fischer—who despite all appearances had been a romantic marshmallow deep inside—had constructed the picture of a couple in love, a couple who simply hadn't yet told anyone else about their feelings. A couple who'd need a place to live and to establish a family. And so, without a word to anyone else of her intentions, she'd called in her lawyer and changed her will....

And the fallout of that decision, Danielle thought wearily, was still drifting over them, with no end in sight.

It was nearly midnight when the last party left the Willows and Danielle could lock up the restaurant and leave. Harry

Evans was still in the office, ostensibly ordering the extra supplies they'd need to have on hand when the strawberry festival began. Danielle knew, however, that he was killing time, waiting around as he always did on the nights it was her turn to close.

She stopped in the office doorway to put on her jacket. "Don't work too late, Dad," she said with only a faint tinge of irony.

Harry shuffled his papers into the desk drawer. "Is it closing time already? I might as well walk out to the lot with you."

Danielle could almost have recited the words along with him. She didn't bother to argue with him anymore. If it made him feel better to stay around to keep a protective eye on his baby and then walk her to her car—well, at least staying up late didn't hurt him the way moving tables did. Harry could sleep well into the morning.

Which was more than Danielle could. She'd have only a few hours to call her own tomorrow, and in that narrow span of time, she'd have to plan the entire weekend. How many guests would be coming in on Friday? How long would they stay? What kind of staples had the Jablonskis left in the kitchen and what would she need to buy?

Despite the hour, the downtown square was still washed with light when Danielle drove through. The shop windows lining the streets glowed softly, showing off merchandise even though there was no one just now to see it. In some of the apartments above—remodeled in the past few years from dark, low-rent rooms into larger, more elaborate homes—windows gleamed. And soft floodlight spilled over the courthouse in the center of the square, making it look even more like a daintily iced wedding cake.

Danielle tried not to look up at Deke's apartment. But it was hard to avoid; it was on the very corner of the square, so rather than just a narrow frontage, his apartment had windows down the entire length, as well.

They were dark, which was no surprise. What had she expected anyway—that he'd be up late pacing the floor and worrying about the Merry Widow? "Maybe fretting because I've taken on so much responsibility and he's doing nothing," she jeered at herself.

But if the square was full of light, two blocks away the Merry Widow was another story. Danielle had never seen the place so utterly black, its windows emptily reflecting the pale moonlight.

She'd intended to put her car away in the carriage house, but the walkway between the buildings was even darker than the house itself. At the last minute, she left the car under the porte cochere. But the key Deke had passed on to her didn't fit the side door, so—grumbling under her breath—she walked around toward the back porch.

High above her was one faint gleam from a tiny attic window that the Jablonskis had no doubt overlooked. The feeble light somehow made the rest of the house seem even darker.

She pushed the back door open. Even though she'd braced herself for the squeal of the hinges, a cold prickle ran up her spine at the sound. Deke hadn't been far wrong when he said the place would make a great haunted house.

"What a comforting thought," Danielle told herself wryly. "Why don't we see if we can conjure up a few spirits while we're at it?"

There was enough moonlight to guide her once her eyes had grown accustomed to the dimness. She'd wait till tomorrow, she decided, to search out the light switches. And she'd run out to the hardware store for some night-lights, too. How had the Jablonskis expected their guests to get around an unfamiliar house in total darkness?

She reached the top of the stairs and paused. She should

have looked around earlier; she hadn't given a thought till just now about which room she should use. The Jablonskis' quarters, she supposed. She'd never been there, but she'd heard Kate talking about fixing up the attic into a private suite so all the more accessible bedrooms were available to guests.

But it hadn't occurred to her to reconnoiter this afternoon. She'd only been thinking of getting away from Deke and that half-mocking smile, that slow and lazy voice. *You utterly amaze me, Danielle....*

She heard a creak from the front of the house, then something that sounded like a long sigh. She froze for an instant and then shook her head and smiled. In a house the size and age of the Merry Widow, creaks would be a dime a dozen. And the sigh was easily explained; the wind had picked up throughout the evening and there was probably no shortage of leaky windows.

She turned toward the set of stairs, only a little narrower and plainer than the main ones, that led up to the attic. She'd been there only once before, on her first inspection tour after Miss Fischer's will was read, and her main impression had been of a single enormous room, full of slanted walls and tiny odd-shaped windows, under the high-peaked roof. The room had been lit only by a few bare bulbs, and there were plenty of boxes stacked haphazardly, most of them clustered in the center around the head of the stairs, as if they'd simply been dumped.

But the huge room Danielle climbed into was nothing at all like the attic she remembered. The basics were still the same; the ceiling soared just as high in the center, and the outer walls still sloped sharply except in the corner tower room.

But there the resemblance ended. The boxes were gone and bright rugs were scattered over the scarred floor. Here and there she thought there was a new wall, blocking off part of the enormous room to create at least the illusion of private space.

Not that she could see much. The only source of light, no doubt the cause of the pale glow she'd seen from outside, was a single small bulb above what looked like a built-in bar in a far corner of the room. No wonder the Jablonskis had missed it; it was so dim that in daylight it probably didn't show up at all.

She was too tired even to walk across the room to turn the light off. She certainly wasn't going to bother to unpack, she decided, or to look for clean sheets. She'd just collapse atop the Jablonskis' bed, and in the morning she'd take care of the details.

Or at least she'd get started.

CHAPTER THREE

DANIELLE was used to waking to sunshine streaming through the wide windows of her father's bungalow. Even on overcast days when there wasn't enough light to rouse her, her internal alarm clock always kicked in, making sure she didn't oversleep.

But on her first morning at the Merry Widow, nothing worked right. There was no sunshine; the Jablonskis had not only selected the darkest attic corner for their bedroom, but they'd angled the privacy wall to close out direct light from the tower windows, the only ones near enough to make a difference. And Danielle's internal clock seemed to be on strike, as well; she felt almost hungover, as if she'd slept far too long—or not nearly long enough.

She must have fallen asleep the moment her head hit the pillow. In fact, Danielle thought wryly as she forced her eyes open, she wasn't so sure her head *had* hit the pillow; all she'd been able to see in the dark room was the corner of the bed, and she'd simply flopped across it and closed her eyes. She felt stiff and lethargic as if she hadn't moved all night. Or perhaps it was still the middle of the night and she'd been jolted into consciousness long before she was ready.

Without even raising her head, she squinted hopefully at the clock on the bedside table and groaned. No such luck—it was morning all right. She'd meant to be awake a couple of hours ago. By now she should have been well on her way to having the Merry Widow organized. Instead...

Something was jabbing at her, poking her in the side. She tugged a book out from under her. It was a hardcover,

40

its jacket wrapped in plastic—no doubt on loan from the local library. In the dim light she could hardly make out the title, but from the design of the cover it was apparently some kind of bloody murder mystery. She wondered if it was Joe or Kate who had the interesting taste in bedtime reading.

She pushed herself up to sit on the edge of the bed. The room was the gloomiest she'd ever known. She was no psychologist, but she wouldn't be a bit surprised if the Jablonskis' fights had something to do with waking up every morning in the dark.

"The first thing I'd do," she muttered, "is knock some skylights into the roof." She tossed the book over her shoulder toward the opposite side of the bed.

It landed with a thump, instantly followed by a growl that sounded to Danielle like a bear with the breath knocked out of him.

The mattress shifted under her, and from the corner of her eye Danielle saw movement to her left, almost behind her. She turned her head so quickly that a muscle in her neck felt as if it had pulled loose completely, and for a moment tears of pain blurred her vision.

"What are you trying to do, knock me unconscious?" Deke asked. There was a faint rasp in his voice this morning. He sounded like warm honey on sandpaper. "And you're on your own with the skylights. Don't send me half of the bill."

Shock turned Danielle's throat as rigid as an icicle. She stared as Deke pushed pillows into a pile against the wall that served as a headboard. She'd never seen him before with the shadow of stubble along his jaw, his eyes dark and still heavy with sleep. The sight sent an almost painful jolt through her, and she hastily looked away from his face, only to see that the soft blanket draping his body had slid to his waist as he leaned back against the pile of pillows, stretching his arms above his head.

Danielle watched the easy ripple of muscle in his bare chest and tried not to remember the last time she'd seen so much of Deke Oliver—at the lake that day after their visit to Miss Fischer. The visit that had seemed so innocent, so casual. The visit that had led directly to this moment.

Though she was damned if she could understand why he was here. He had a perfectly good apartment, and she'd have sworn the last thing he'd intended when they parted yesterday was to get further involved with the Merry Widow.

"All the persuasive energy I exerted trying to get you into bed went for nothing," Deke mused. "And now, with no effort at all, here we are. Ironic, isn't it?"

Fury melted the icicle in Danielle's throat. "So that's it. You saw your chance—"

"And rushed right over so I could experience the dubious pleasure of waking up beside you?" Deke said, frowning. "Hardly."

Danielle gulped. It did sound pretty stupid, phrased that way.

"And your salacious scenario has another small problem, too," Deke continued relentlessly. "I could hardly have planned this—exciting though it is to sit here in bed and argue with you—because I had no idea you were actually planning to move in. What are you doing here anyway?"

Danielle tried to think through the conversation they'd had yesterday. Had she said anything then about her intentions of staying at the Merry Widow? She couldn't remember, so she went on the attack instead. "It looks to me as if you're the one who's taken up residence."

"But you brought a suitcase." Deke pointed to her luggage, where she'd dumped it at the foot of the bed. "I have only the clothes on my back. Figuratively speaking."

With all the self-control in her command, Danielle couldn't stop her gaze from drifting down the length of his body. The soft blanket draped intimately around him, making it obvious that the only thing he was wearing was a wristwatch.

Feeling herself grow warm, she forced her gaze away from him and her attention back to the problem. "So why *are* you here?"

A voice echoed up the stairwell. "Hello up there! Anybody home?"

Danielle's eyes widened. "You're entertaining here instead of in your own apartment? If I'd known I'd walked into a rendezvous—"

"This is not a rendezvous," Deke said mildly. "And that is Mrs. Winslow. Otherwise known—along with her husband—as my reason for being here." He glanced at his watch, a gold slash against his tanned skin. "And she's looking for breakfast."

"I don't get it. You mean they're guests? But there wasn't anything in the reservations book."

"Certain of that, are you?" Deke pushed the blanket back.

Danielle averted her eyes and tried to remember what she'd read in the reservations book. *Was* she certain? She could see the calendar in her mind—but it was open to the strawberry festival, not the current week. "Not absolutely," she admitted.

"Well, you're right. Their reservation is for today—but they arrived a full twenty-four hours early, just as I was leaving the house yesterday. And since I had no idea how you planned to handle the details—whether, for instance, you intended to pass out keys so guests can come and go as they please or just leave the place standing wide open…"

Danielle flung herself against the pillows and started to

chuckle. "So you've been held hostage overnight? Poor Deke! Serves you right for laughing at me. If you hadn't, I'd probably still have been here when they arrived and you could have ducked out."

The cheerful voice called again, and an instant later a head topped with frizzy gray hair popped around the end of the privacy wall. The woman's gaze slid from Deke, who was just starting to zip his trousers, to Danielle—still sprawled across the bed—and back.

"Oh, my," Mrs. Winslow said faintly. "No wonder you weren't answering earlier. I do beg your pardon." She disappeared, and footsteps retreated hastily toward the stairs.

All Danielle's desire to laugh had abruptly evaporated.

Deke put on his shirt. "Well, since you're here, you can take on the breakfast detail."

"Nice try." Danielle pushed herself up from the bed. "You could have warned me last night, you know. So, since you didn't, make their breakfast yourself."

"And have them sue over the cooking? Besides, I tried to warn you. I called the Willows twice last night. Once I got cut off, and the other time I was on hold till my ear was black and blue."

"We had a lot of parties last night," Danielle admitted. "Nobody had time to answer phones and carry notes."

"That was apparent. Then I left a message on the machine at your father's house, but obviously you didn't get it."

"I came straight here after work. And since Dad knew where I was going…"

Deke nodded. "He probably thought there was no point in calling since I said I'd wait here for you."

Danielle pounced. "So you did expect that I'd come and you set up a booby trap for me."

Deke turned slowly to face her. Very deliberately, he fastened the last button on his shirt, folded the cuffs back halfway to his elbows and tucked the tail neatly into the waistband of his trousers. "If by a booby trap, you mean you think I plotted some sort of seduction scene, Danielle..."

She'd spoken without thinking, and now an almost painful flush rose from throat to forehead.

"If I'd had any such intention, I'd certainly have stayed awake for the payoff." His voice was dry. "As it happens, I got tired of waiting and of Joe's taste in literature, and decided to get some sleep. I didn't even hear you come in."

And since she hadn't turned on a light...

"Good thing I didn't choose the other side of the bed," Danielle said wryly.

"Isn't it, though?"

Danielle stared at him, eyes narrowed in suspicion. "Look, if you think I saw you here and climbed in just for the sheer joy of sleeping with you... I've met some egos in my day, Oliver, but you take the—"

"The possibility never occurred to me."

She was relieved, though still a bit wary. "That's something, I suppose."

"Because if that was what you wanted, you'd have made sure I woke up." The last of the sandpaper roughness was gone from his voice; it was pure honey now. Warm honey, which seemed to ooze through her skin and trickle into her veins... "Which makes us even, doesn't it?"

You can't win, she told herself. *And you're an idiot to keep trying.*

She turned on her heel, circled the end of the privacy wall and descended the stairs all the way to the kitchen. She knew perfectly well Deke was right behind her, almost in perfect step, but she wasn't going to give him the satisfaction of any further reactions.

At the bottom of the stairs, he murmured, "You wouldn't

like to walk up again, would you? I'll bet your skirt's even more attractive from that angle.''

She tried to ignore him; Deke was chuckling as she opened the kitchen door.

The room smelled of coffee and frying ham. At the stove, Mrs. Winslow was carefully forking thick slices of meat from a skillet onto a couple of plates. Nearby, a bald man with thick glasses was buttering toast.

Mrs. Winslow grinned over her shoulder at Danielle and Deke. "I thought—under the circumstances—that you wouldn't mind us helping ourselves. Want some ham and eggs?''

Danielle, absolutely speechless, shook her head.

Deke said, "Sounds wonderful to me. Can I pour you some coffee, my dear?''

Mrs. Winslow gave him an approving nod. "That's the style. Take good care of her. Hand me the basket of eggs, Bill.''

Danielle would have liked to refuse the mug Deke handed her, but she needed the caffeine. She stood back to watch as Mrs. Winslow expertly cracked two eggs against the edge of the skillet and tossed the shells aside.

"You don't keep much variety in this kitchen, do you? But I guess," the woman added generously, "you weren't expecting company quite so soon. And it seems that honeymooners always forget about eating if someone doesn't remind them.''

Danielle choked on her first mouthful of coffee.

Deke said gently, "Oh, we're not honeymooners. In fact, we're not even—''

"We're just new to the bed-and-breakfast trade," Danielle cut in. "Give us a few days to get into the rhythm of things and you'll be amazed at what we can do.''

"My thoughts exactly," Deke murmured. "Of course, I'm already amazed at you, sweetheart.''

She glared at him. Deke raised an eyebrow and smiled back. When Mr. Winslow snickered, it was the last straw for Danielle. She set her coffee mug gently on the counter. "Since you seem to have everything under control here, *darling*," she said sweetly, "I'll go start preparing for the guests who'll be coming this afternoon." She didn't pause for a reaction and managed—by gritting her teeth—to wait till she was in the front parlor, at the far corner of the house, before she gave in to the urge to kick something.

She only wished that instead of an upholstered hassock, it had been Deke.

The reservations book said there would be two families checking in on Friday, and Kate had noted in her tiny, precise script that both would arrive in the late afternoon. Danielle hoped she was right about the times, but after the Winslows' early appearance, she was a bit gun-shy.

She'd known all along that running the Merry Widow on top of her regular job wasn't going to be any picnic, but she'd obviously miscalculated the extent of the difficulty. After digging through the Jablonskis' desk, she'd found an extra key for the Winslows, so while she was at work they could get back into the Merry Widow after visiting with the friends they'd come to see in Elmwood. But what about tomorrow? Was she going to have to provide keys to two more sets of guests? How was she supposed to keep track of who returned them? What happened if some careless guest lost one?

At this rate, she reflected, the locksmith stood to make more off the Merry Widow than anyone else was going to.

She stared across the main dining room of the Willows, but she was seeing a phantom grocery list in her mind. Her experience was with the service end of the restaurant business; though she'd bought food for crowds, preparing it was something else. And the weekend's guests included three children. She'd be lucky if all three didn't have picky appetites. Would there be time to start a batch of sticky rolls tonight after the dinner rush? Or should she confine herself to something simpler? Muffins, perhaps. Since the Willows was closed for lunch on Saturday, she wouldn't have to be at work till the dinner hour—

"Are you going to answer that telephone," Pam said, "or just stand there and let it ring?"

Danielle jumped, but by the time she'd picked up the phone, whoever was on the other end had given up. That reminded her of the night before. If Deke had really tried to get through to tell her about the Winslows' arrival...

The only reason she was concerned, Danielle told herself, was that they could be missing important business that way. People wanting to book tables or schedule parties...

Pam substituted a new cash drawer, freshly loaded with change, and picked up the old one. Instead of carrying it back to the office to sort out the bank deposit, however, she tipped her head to one side and inspected Danielle. "You already look frazzled. If half the talk going around town is accurate, I'm not surprised."

Danielle froze. "What's everyone saying?"

"I was teasing, Danny. Since when did you pay any attention to what the gossips are going on about?" Pam looked puzzled. "You don't mean there's really something to it all?"

"Well, that depends on what the story is, doesn't it?"

"You mean you want to hear it? The most recent version is that Joe Jablonski left a message for Deke with one of the clerks at the antique shop on the square, downstairs from Deke's apartment."

"Amazing. They've got it right so far."

"The clerk told the owner all about it, and she told the ringleader of the gossips—"

"Mrs. Hansen is in on this?" Danielle rolled her eyes.

"You expected her to stay out of such a juicy story? The way I heard it, the Merry Widow is full of termites, and that's why Joe and Kate gave up on it. Of course, it was Deke who planted the termites—"

"Now *that* sounds almost reasonable."

"Because Joe was blackmailing him over something or other. Nobody seems to know what."

"If they knew," Danielle pointed out, "it would no longer be blackmail material."

"Well, maybe that's why Joe finally called it quits, if it wasn't going to benefit him anymore. It's a known fact—" Pam opened her eyes very wide for emphasis "—that when Deke heard about Joe's leaving town, he threatened to hunt him down and break his knees."

Danielle pressed a fingertip to the center of her forehead and closed her eyes, trying to follow the logic. "Wait a minute. I'd think Deke would be delighted to see the last of the blackmailer."

"Well, I thought it sounded suspiciously like the last Mafia movie I saw," Pam admitted, "but you have to give Mrs. Hansen credit. She's a natural when it comes to high-concept fiction."

Danielle relaxed. "In other words, the gossip is all the usual stuff." She smiled at her own overreaction. For a minute there, she'd actually wondered if one of the town's busybodies might have tuned her antenna just right to pick up on this morning's craziness. Which was ridiculous, of course; she was just supersensitive at the moment.

Pam's eyebrows arched. "You expected worse than blackmail, a crumbling house and threats of bodily injury? That must mean there's something *really* going on." She put the cash drawer on the counter and planted her elbows on it. "Come on, Danny, you can't leave me hanging like this!"

The main door opened, and with relief Danielle turned

to greet the new customers. Her smile froze as she recognized Mrs. Winslow's frizzy gray hair. But even worse, the woman with Mrs. Winslow was the one Pam called the ringleader of all Elmwood's gossips.

Suddenly, Danielle knew exactly how it would feel to stand on a guillotine platform, awaiting the executioner's convenience.

She swallowed hard and stepped forward. "Good afternoon, ladies. A table for two?"

"Four, please," Mrs. Hansen cooed. "The men are parking the car. It's good to see you looking so lovely, Danielle, dear. Have you found a new beauty secret? You're absolutely blooming."

"Thank you," Danielle said dutifully. The guillotine blade was about to drop; she knew it, and there wasn't a thing she could do to prevent it.

Mrs. Winslow was almost jumping up and down with pleasure. "But of course she has, with that handsome husband of hers taking such good care of her! Danielle—what a pretty name. I was so busy with breakfast this morning that I didn't think to ask."

"Husband?" Mrs. Hansen's voice remained calm, but her gaze sharpened. "Danielle's not married. What made you think she is?"

Mrs. Winslow's smile slowly faded. "But she and Deke—Mr. Oliver—were both...they were..."

Pam was leaning so far over the counter she lost her balance and almost pushed the full cash drawer off onto the floor. "Oh, please don't stop now," she begged.

Danielle told herself the best she could hope for was damage control. "I think there's been a—"

"They were in bed together." Mrs. Winslow's voice had dropped to a horrified whisper. "So *of course* I assumed they were married."

Pam's jaw sagged, and her eyes looked as big as plates.

Danielle pasted a smile on her face. "A natural conclusion," she said gently. "Though I have to tell you that in fact, if Deke Oliver was the last man on the face of the earth…"

Pam was still staring blankly at her, but Danielle knew it wouldn't be long before her friend's shock seeped away to be replaced with suspicion.

Be careful not to protest too much, Danielle warned herself. *That's exactly the sort of thing the rejected woman would say. It isn't going to convince Mrs. Hansen—and it'll no doubt start Pam wondering, too.*

The main door opened behind her. The car-parking contingent, Danielle thought, and she didn't turn around. She looked straight at Pam instead. "Well, I suppose if he *was* the last male on the face of the earth…" She shook her head. "No, even that wouldn't make Deke Oliver a marriageable sort of man."

Pam's voice dripped skepticism. "So you're just sleeping with him instead?" Her gaze focused on a spot slightly above and behind Danielle's head.

Danielle's heart started to beat a little faster and the hairs on the back of her neck stood on end, as if there was an electrical current surging through the air. *Great*, she thought. *Why couldn't my warning system have worked last night, when it would have done some good?*

Deke's voice was as warm and smooth as melted butter. "At the risk of sounding immodest, I'm sure Danielle finds the experience unforgettable."

How does he do that? Danielle asked herself frantically. *Let everyone in the place hear him and still sound as intimate as if he's whispering naughty phrases in my ear.* "Not from lack of trying, I assure you."

"Careful, sweetheart, you'll bruise my ego."

"If only that was possible," Danielle said sweetly. "Ladies, if you'll follow me, I'll show you to the solarium.'' When she returned, the foyer was empty. Danielle leaned against the door of the office and watched as Pam, sitting at Harry's desk, sorted out the cash drawer. ''No Deke?''

''Don't get a big head,'' Pam advised without looking up. ''You didn't drive him off. Your father seated him in the dining room.''

''I didn't think I could be lucky enough that he'd leave.''

Pam sat back in her chair. ''Danielle—''

''I'm not sleeping with him, Pam. At least—well, yes, I did, but it was hardly...''

Pam was shaking her head. ''I really don't want the details. And it doesn't matter, you know, whether you are or not. Now that Mrs. Hansen has her teeth into that story, she won't let go.''

''So I might as well relax and enjoy it, right?'' Danielle said dryly. She straightened the list of table bookings on the stand by the main door and tried not to think about the past few minutes.

Fifteen years ago, when as a mere child she'd started busing tables in the restaurant, she'd learned the hard way not to discuss her personal business or her feelings with or in front of customers. Well, that little rule had gone down the drain in a hurry today. Within the hour, all of Elmwood would have heard that Danielle Evans and Deke Oliver had been caught in bed together.

And, she reminded herself, it wouldn't take much longer for everyone to hear that they were sniping at each other about it, too. Which would only make the entire tale more deliciously believable.

She leaned around the corner into the office. ''Pam, could you keep an eye on things for a bit? Harry's in the lounge if it gets busy.''

Pam nodded. ''I have to be out of here by two, though,'' she warned. ''Jessica has a piano lesson right after school.''

"It shouldn't take nearly that long." Before she could lose her nerve, Danielle strolled into the dining room. Once again, Deke was at the corner table; the waitress was just setting a plate before him.

Danielle pulled out a chair and sat down.

Deke didn't turn a hair. "What a pleasant surprise. May I buy you lunch?"

"Just a cup of tea, please, Sally," Danielle told the waitress.

"Nothing more?" Deke asked. "Then I hope you don't mind if I eat. Your father's Philly-steak sandwich is too good to pass up."

The waitress was back with Danielle's tea before he said another word. Danielle toyed with her cup and finally asked, "Aren't you even curious about why I'm here?"

"Oh, no. Now that you've made it quite plain that you aren't trying to marry me—"

Danielle saw red. "And I never was, either. No matter what you thought, I did not put Miss Fischer up to anything. It was entirely her own idea that inheriting a house together would propel us toward matrimony, and if she'd ever discussed it with me, I'd have told her—"

"Is that what you wanted to talk about?" Deke's eyebrows had risen slightly. "Personally, I'm a bit tired of the discussion."

"I'm sure you are, since you were dead wrong and you know it." Danielle took three deep breaths. "But that's not why I'm here. The whole thing this morning is a comedy of errors. If we treat it like the funny story it is, it'll go away in a few days. People will find something else to talk about, and—"

"Why would I want it to go away?"

"Oh, come on. Deke, the great uncommitted?"

"Exactly. Everybody in town now knows that we've

agreed not to be serious. So why shouldn't we enjoy our-selves?"

Danielle stared at him. Was the man for real?

"I don't see why you want nothing to do with me. We're a great combination—now that you understand there's nothing permanent about it."

"I not only understand that, Deke, I'm glad of it."

"Then what's the big deal? We had fun together—and we could again." He reached for her hand.

Danielle moved it, but not quite fast enough; Deke's fingertips stroked the tendons in the back of her hand. She felt as if he'd reached under the skin and twisted each separate nerve.

"I've missed you, you know," he said. "And since we've got things straightened out—"

Above her, a man cleared his throat. "Excuse me," he said. "You're the ones to talk to now about the Merry Widow, aren't you? The new owners?"

Danielle turned to look up at him. She recognized the face; he was often at the Willows during the lunch hour, always in work clothes. But she'd never known his name.

"Not exactly," she said finally.

"Well, I've got that bid ready." He obviously saw the lack of comprehension in her face and elaborated, "The final figures on the roof work."

"It's just too perfect," Deke said under his breath. "The roof is caving in. I should've guessed."

"Oh, no," the workman assured him. "It's not in that bad a shape. But it's not something that can be put off, either. There's already a leak in the back wing, you know, and it's only going to get worse." He pulled a creased and worn sheet of paper from his hip pocket and handed it to Deke with a flourish. "Just let me know when you're ready, and I'll work you into the schedule." He grinned and went off, whistling.

Danielle put her hands to her temples. "How much?"

"Two thousand six hundred."

"So I have to come up with thirteen hundred dollars by..." She shook her head. "I can't do it, Deke."

"I meant that's your share. The whole bill's over five grand." Deke tossed the paper down beside his plate. "Are you *certain* you don't just want to burn the place down, Danielle?"

CHAPTER FOUR

TWENTY-SIX hundred dollars. And Danielle didn't have a cent of it.

Deke finished his sandwich and salad, gave due consideration to the tray of elaborate desserts the waitress displayed for him, shook his head, then settled back with a cup of coffee. Though he hadn't uttered a word to Danielle, his silence wasn't tense or challenging or abrasive; he'd obviously said everything he intended to and was simply letting her think.

Not that time was doing Danielle any good. She could contemplate well into next year and still not have that kind of cash in her possession. And even if she could snap her fingers and create twenty-six hundred dollars, she'd hardly be out of the woods; she wasn't naive enough to think that the cost of fixing a leaky roof would be the last bill coming to roost at the Merry Widow.

She could ask her father for the money, of course. In the months since she'd come home to help at the Willows, Danielle hadn't actually drawn a regular salary. Since she'd always expected to be going back to school in the near future, she'd just taken a cash advance once in a while to meet her few expenses.

So Harry would certainly understand why she didn't have that kind of money on hand, and there was no doubt in Danielle's mind that he'd help her out. But she didn't want to ask. She'd come home to help by taking on part of Harry's load—not add to it by creating bills for him to pay.

She could ask him to lend her the money, but calling it

a loan wouldn't make it one. She couldn't pay it back soon—at least not till the Merry Widow was sold, and there was no guarantee of when that would be. To accept Harry's help as a gift...she absolutely wouldn't do it.

But if it came down to telling Deke that she simply couldn't meet her obligations...

What other choice did she have?

Danielle cleared her throat. "I'll have to apply for a bank loan," she said without looking at him. "And since the only thing I have to offer as security is my half of the Merry Widow, I suppose that means you'll have to agree to the loan terms."

Deke was silent for so long that she wasn't sure he'd heard. Then he said, "I don't like the idea much. Taking on debt on a property of questionable value is like borrowing money to invest in a pyramid scheme. What happened to your share of the house payments?"

Danielle knew she should have expected the question; he'd brought it up once before, and she ought to have known he wouldn't let it drop. She said stiffly, "I put that money to very good use."

"I'm certain you did." Irony oozed from Deke's voice. "And—no doubt—that's why you can't get at any of it now."

"It's not precisely a liquid investment, no."

Deke nodded. "It's the lottery, isn't it?"

"I beg your pardon? I don't know what you..." Light dawned, followed by instant fury. "No, I haven't spent my share of the Jablonskis' money on lottery tickets, thank you very much for your confidence! And if you're going to tell me that you've still got the first dollar of your share stashed away in some money market fund—"

"As a matter of fact," Deke said coolly, "that's exactly where it is."

"Well, that does suggest an answer. If you don't like

having a bank involved, Deke, why don't you make me the loan? You'll get your money back out of my share of the profits when the Merry Widow sells.''

"*If* it sells. And *if* there are profits.'' Deke glanced at the charge slip the waitress had set beside him, signed it and pushed his chair back. "Sorry I can't pursue the discussion just now, but I have an appointment. What shall I tell the roofer, Danielle?''

That before we sign a contract, I need to have a fast talk with Rumpelstiltskin, Danielle thought. "Can I at least have a while to consider my options?''

"Of course,'' Deke murmured. "Take all the time you want. Last night when I watched the weather forecast, there was no rain predicted till the middle of next week, so with any luck we won't have a river running through the Merry Widow for a few days at least.''

Though Friday evenings were always busy at the Willows, a rash of special parties kept Danielle on her toes even more than usual that night. Both she and Harry were constantly busy greeting diners and assigning waitresses and juggling seating arrangements, and still there was a line of people in the lobby waiting for tables.

But all the while, behind her smile and small talk, Danielle was considering the matter of the Merry Widow's roof, worrying at it like a puppy with a too big bone—and like the puppy, getting precisely nowhere.

Just as Harry took the last waiting group to their table and Danielle thought she could finally take a deep breath, the door opened once more. Among the half-dozen people who came in, bringing laughter and cool night air and the scent of buttered popcorn with them, were Pam and Greg Lanning.

Popcorn? Danielle wondered. Had Pam said something about going to a movie tonight? "It'll be about twenty minutes before I'll have a table for you,'' she warned. ''If you'd like to wait in the lounge—''

''I'll wait anywhere as long as you don't try to put me to work,'' Pam said frankly.

''I could find plenty for you to do,'' Danielle admitted. Pam laughed and led the way toward the lounge.

At the back of the group, a lanky young man fell behind the rest and stopped beside the maître d's stand. ''Hello, Danielle. I've been hearing some interesting gossip.''

He sounded more sad than meddlesome, but still annoyance sizzled through Danielle's veins. ''Well, it *is* Elmwood, Kevin. You can hear pretty much anything in this town if you listen long enough.''

He smiled, his face lighting up as if the sun had risen in his eyes. ''It's not true, then? I didn't think it could be. You're going to Pam's party Sunday, aren't you?''

''I'm planning to.'' Danielle's tone was cautious. *And if you ask me to go with you, Kevin, the answer's going to be the same as it's been for the past six months*. Because no matter how much she'd like to make it plain to the entire town that she and Deke were not an item—and showing up at Pam's party with a date would go a long way toward making the point—it would be terribly unfair to Kevin if she used him that way.

And if the noble reason wasn't enough to make her refuse, she reminded herself, there was always the less noble one. Poor Kevin; she'd gone out with him only twice, but it had taken nearly half a year to convince him that she could never see him as anything but a friend. If she gave him the slightest bit of encouragement now—

''I'll see you there, then,'' he said cheerfully, and followed Pam's group into the lounge.

Danielle stood absolutely still for an instant, then shook her head and smiled wryly at her own egotism. Thank heaven she hadn't actually refused an invitation that he'd apparently had no intention of issuing. Poor Kevin indeed!

Harry came back to the main lobby, gave a gusty sigh of relief when he saw the empty benches and pulled out a big handkerchief to mop his forehead.

Danielle watched him with concern. He'd been working hard, yes—they all had. But the Willows wasn't that warm. The vague notion she'd had of asking Harry for advice on where to get a loan vanished in concern for her father. "Dad, go home and get some rest. Better yet, go lie down in the office till I can get someone to take you home."

Harry scoffed. "I'm fine. How would it look if I folded up under the pressure of walking people to their tables and had to run home to recuperate?"

"Like you were taking care of yourself for a change."

Harry smiled. "Tell you what," he offered. "I'll lie down till the crowd starts to leave. Will that keep you happy?"

"If it's all I can get," Danielle muttered.

And he *did* look much better by the time the last diners had left, she thought. Tired, of course, as they all were. But as he walked her out to her car, he even teased Danielle about treating him like a baby. Neither the teasing nor the complaint stopped her from following him home, just to be sure he got there safely.

The Merry Widow couldn't have looked more different than it had the night before, Danielle reflected as she parked her car in the small courtyard behind the house. Lights gleamed in almost every bedroom window, and the main rooms were aglow, as well.

Just what I need, Danielle thought. *A bunch of party people.*

She reminded herself that as long as her guests paid the rates, they were entitled to act however they liked as long as they didn't disturb the other guests. It was probably too much to ask that they not disturb the manager, she mused with a tinge of irony.

She glanced at the kitchen clock and gave up the idea of sticky rolls for tomorrow's breakfast. If she managed to stay awake while she waited for the dough to rise, she wouldn't be alert enough even to make coffee in the morning. And if she didn't—well, she'd have enough to do tomorrow without cleaning up the mess an uncontrolled batch of yeast dough would make of the kitchen.

She was measuring the ingredients for a coffee cake when the door between the kitchen and butler's pantry swung open. She looked over her shoulder, expecting to see one of the three juvenile guests, and dumped an extra spoonful of baking powder into the bowl when she saw Deke instead. "I didn't see your car out there," she said, and felt instantly foolish. She hadn't seen it last night, either.

"I walked over. Of course if I'd realized you were going to work late again and I'd have to risk crossing the square at this hour, all alone in the dark—"

"The odds of getting mugged in Elmwood are about the same as being struck by lightning *and* abducted by aliens in the same day. So if you're hinting for an invitation to stay, forget it."

"With both of us awake, it would certainly be more interesting than last night. But I wasn't hinting, just hanging around keeping an eye on things."

Danielle stirred the dry ingredients together and kept stirring. "Thanks," she said finally, her voice a bit gruff. "Having all those kids here made me think twice about leaving."

"I thought it would be wise not to take any unnecessary chances," Deke agreed. "Now that we're going to have an even larger investment than we expected…"

Danielle dropped her spoon. "You mean the roof? Or has something else gone bad?"

"Not just yet. The good news is, the estimate for the roof repair is low, considering the amount of work that needs to be done."

"That's good? All right, I guess it could be worse."

"But the contractor's right. It can't be ignored or we won't just have a leaky roof, we'll have waterfalls in the bedrooms."

"Well, that would be sort of an elegant touch, don't you think? A fountain in each room?"

"However," Deke went on, "he's agreed to accept payments over several months. So I gave him a check for the first part, and he's going to start work as soon as he can."

Danielle swallowed hard. "I—thanks, Deke. I'll take care of my share." *Somehow.*

"And I talked to a lawyer about making sure we don't get stuck with the bill if the Jablonskis come back."

"I thought you were certain they'd left for good."

"I still think so. I just believe in being careful."

Danielle couldn't help it. "Oh, there's never been any doubt of that," she murmured. "You being careful, that is."

She covered the bowl with plastic wrap and set it aside with the cookbook open next to it. First thing in the morning, she'd add the milk and eggs and put the coffee cake in the oven, and with any luck it would be ready by the time the guests came down. With coffee and tea and juice, and the fresh fruit she'd bought this morning…

Deke was being awfully quiet, she noticed. Of course, that wisecrack *had* been a bit much; the man had just given her a reprieve on a very large debt. She glanced at him. He was leaning casually against the counter only a couple of feet from her, arms folded, watching with apparent absorption as she worked.

But though he appeared to be perfectly at ease, the air around him seemed to throb with energy. Low-level energy, she thought. It wasn't like being caught in an electrical storm, Danielle realized, but the quiet beforehand, when the tension was building in a slow upward spiral toward the inevitable discharge.

Just the way she'd felt in the moments before he'd kissed her for the first time all those months ago....

And that, Danielle told herself, *is enough of that. He's not going to do it again, and if he tried, you wouldn't let him...would you?*

Deke moved a fraction closer. ''By the way, now that I've had a chance to think about it, I rather like your idea.''

The casual note in his voice soaked up all the tension like a cotton ball in water, leaving Danielle feeling dazed at the sudden change. ''Which idea?'' she asked faintly.

''About how our being friends will defuse all the talk.''

She frowned. ''That's not exactly what I...'' She paused, then tried again. ''Deke, all I said is that we should laugh it off like the joke it is.''

He nodded. ''Exactly—and we can't do that if we're avoiding each other or taking swipes whenever we get a chance. That's what you meant, isn't it?''

She couldn't deny it; that was precisely what she'd had in mind when she strolled into the dining room of the Willows today and took a seat at his table. But she hadn't thought of it quite in terms of *friendship*.

''And the really great thing about it,'' Deke murmured, ''is that acting that way leaves us free to do exactly as we like.'' He touched the tip of his index finger to her nose and smiled down into her eyes. ''So, my dear—am I staying here tonight or going home?''

In the end, he left. But Danielle had a sneaking suspicion he'd never intended to stay, that the whole question had been merely a source of amusement, an opportunity to enjoy listening to her stammer. *Why* hadn't she been able to tell him coolly to cut out the nonsense and go away?

Surely it didn't have anything to do with what had happened that morning when she'd awakened next to him. She wasn't foolish enough to forget everything else she knew about Deke Oliver just because the man had turned out to be even sexier than she'd ever imagined. Warm and tousled, with a shadow of stubble and a sleep-rasped voice...

The man didn't just have bedroom eyes. He had a bedroom *body*, for heaven's sake.

But that didn't mean she'd lost all her common sense.

She was telling herself that once more, in the early hours of Saturday morning as she was pulling on blue jeans and a striped blouse, when the telephone rang beside the Jablonskis' bed. She picked it up doubtfully. "The Merry Widow."

Deke said, "You don't sound very merry this morning."

"You wouldn't be, either," Danielle grumbled, "if you'd just had a cold shower."

"I'm amazed you could wait so long. I had one last night right after I got home."

Danielle was glad he wasn't there to see the hot color rise in her face. "Mine was not deliberate, so don't flatter yourself. There's no hot water up here this morning."

"Let's hope there is in the rest of the house."

Danielle closed her eyes in pain. "That possibility hadn't even occurred to me. Are you calling about something important? Because I really should be checking on the water supply instead of chatting."

"I was only making sure you were up. After yesterday, it seemed like a good idea—unless you want Mrs. Winslow to make breakfast again."

"I've already had to give them a rebate on their first

night's stay because of that, so yes, I'd like to beat her to the kitchen this morning. And since I'm up and ready—''

"And I also called to see if you need eggs or anything like that. I'll be happy to bring them right over."

Danielle squinted at her watch. "It's six in the morning, Deke."

"I know."

"What are you doing? Confirming for the gossips that we can't stand being apart?"

"Exactly. How brilliant of you to notice. That's why, when I came back last night, I was very careful not to turn on any lights—so nobody would know I was home."

"So they'd assume you were here instead? You know, Deke, we could switch places. *You* can stay here nights and enjoy cold showers, and I'll go home."

"You can't expect to have everything perfect just because it's the penthouse, darling."

The penthouse? That wasn't exactly what Danielle would call it, but she wasn't about to stay on the phone and discuss it. As a matter of fact, the Jablonskis' suite could be cute as a bug. With a whole lot more light and the right decorating scheme to play up its unique features, the attic might even be worthy of being called a penthouse.

But it would never be spacious or private. Even the bedroom wasn't completely walled off from the rest of the living quarters, and any sound seemed to echo off the high ceilings and vibrate through the entire apartment. For a couple already having difficulties, the tight quarters would have been an additional irritant.

Of course, it wasn't as if the Jablonskis were confined to the small, dark space. They had the rest of the Merry Widow to relax in—at least as much as one could relax with a half-dozen guests around. Danielle hadn't yet acquired the knack. She wasn't so sure it was a skill one could learn.

Breakfast lived up to her worst expectations. One of the teenage guests turned up her nose at the coffee cake—too much sugar, she said—and asked for melba toast instead. The smaller children announced that they did not like fruit and ate most of the coffee cake before the last of the guests had even come downstairs. Danielle made a mental note to divide tomorrow's breakfast into two batches and hide one for the latecomers.

The Winslows, with a few sly looks but no overt comments, went off to spend the day with their friends. One family headed for the lake while the other went antiquing. And with the Merry Widow empty, Danielle pulled out a chair, poured herself a cup of coffee and sampled the remaining crumbs of the coffee cake.

She was drained, and the day had only started. There were beds to be changed, baths to be cleaned, the public rooms to be dusted and vacuumed. There were sheets and towels to be laundered, tomorrow's breakfast to plan, the grocery shopping to do.

She put the dirty dishes to soak in the kitchen sink—why the Jablonskis hadn't invested in a dishwasher was anybody's guess—picked up the mail from beneath the slot in the front door and dumped the envelopes atop the stack from yesterday. Most, she thought, looked like bills—and just now, she couldn't face them.

Danielle reached for a sweater and stepped out into the sunshine. Since it was Saturday and the Willows would be closed during the lunch hour, she could afford to take an hour for herself before she plunged into the waiting work. And she was going to enjoy every second of it.

If it wasn't for a still-crisp breeze that teased at her hair and ran a chilly finger down her neck, Danielle wouldn't have needed the sweater, for the sun lay warm on her skin as she strolled down Harrison Street toward the square at the center of town. The last of the tulips nodded in the breeze as if greeting her, while lilacs scented the air and an early peony peeked around a sunny corner.

The square was busy, even for a Saturday. Most of the shops and boutiques lining the streets had propped their front doors open, an invitation both to customers and to the pleasant weather. Danielle waved at a couple of friends, but she didn't stop till she reached a wide old storefront on the far side of the square, the home of the county historical museum.

The white-haired president of the museum society was crouched in the front window, dusting and arranging the re-creation of an early Elmwood general store. She grimaced at Danielle and made frantic beckoning gestures.

Danielle dug her museum key from deep in her jeans pocket, unlocked the door and went in. "What's wrong, Martha?"

"Not a thing, except I got myself in here and I can't seem to get turned around so I can climb out."

Danielle could see the problem; the window was stuffed with merchandise, just the way an early retailer would have displayed his goods to draw the public's interest, and Martha was standing in the only empty spot, barely a foot square. Danielle climbed the utility ladder that stood by the ledge at the back of the window and reached in to offer her arm for Martha to use for balance. "How'd you get in there?"

"If I knew, I could've just got out the reverse way," Martha said tartly. "I just started to dust, and before I knew it, here I was. Hand me that lantern, would you? Now that I've got this space cleared out for it, it'd be a shame to leave a hole right in the middle of the display."

Danielle passed her a tin lantern, obviously old but in almost mint condition, and Martha settled it in the infinitesimal space between her feet. She dusted off her hands and leaned heavily on Danielle's arm as she did a sort of vertical limbo around a dress form.

Once safely on the ledge at the back of the window, Martha took a deep breath and grinned. "I don't mind telling you I'm glad to see you. Most people thought I was just waving, and the two who knew better didn't have keys. They're probably looking for a phone so they can call you to come and rescue me."

Danielle shook her head. Martha was as stubborn in her own way as Danielle's father was, and talking to her did just about as much good as trying to persuade Harry Evans. She knew she might as well save her breath, but she couldn't live with herself if something happened to Martha and she hadn't tried to prevent it. "You realize it's dangerous for you to be climbing around in here, alone, with the doors locked. What if you'd been toward the back where no one could see you?"

Martha bounded down from the ledge. "Then you'd have found me when you came inside," she said comfortably. "There's another stack of oral history tapes for you. Bill brought them in just yesterday. Said he'd been out to the retirement home and got several interesting stories."

"That's great, Martha." Danielle tried again. "You know, now that the museum has a little extra money, maybe we could hire somebody to dust and polish."

Martha shook her head. "That money isn't exactly extra. It was given with restrictions—only the interest can be used to run the museum. And since the donor's anonymous, we can't exactly ask if it's okay to change the rules, can we?"

Danielle bit her tongue. *Caught in my own net*, she thought.

The whole concept of remaining anonymous had seemed such a good idea eight months ago when she'd cashed the Jablonskis' first check, wrapped the bills into a neatly typed letter and mailed the packet to Martha at the museum.

Anonymity had several advantages, but the main one was not having to explain to every interested party in Elmwood precisely why she'd chosen to donate the proceeds from the Merry Widow's sale. The last thing she needed was for Elmwood to start speculating on questions like whether her guilty conscience was because of selling Miss Fischer's house or inheriting it in the first place.

She managed to keep her voice even. "I'm only talking about a few hours a month. I'd think the interest would cover what I'm talking about."

"Probably, but I think it's wiser to leave the interest alone and let the fund grow a bit."

Danielle could hardly argue. It *was* a sensible decision, especially now that there wouldn't be any additional contributions to the fund for the foreseeable future. Of course, Martha didn't know that yet—and Danielle wasn't supposed to know, either, she reminded herself.

"With the Merry Widow on the market again…" Martha began.

Danielle felt her muscles stiffen. What had brought that particular subject to Martha's mind? she wondered. Did she suspect the origin of that special fund with its irregular cash donations? And how many other people might, as well—especially now that the fund's status would change right along with the Merry Widow's?

"I don't suppose you'll have time to do another workshop on how to interview people for oral histories," Martha went on. "You must have your hands downright full at the moment."

"You could say that." Relief trickled through Danielle's body. It had been an innocent question after all, a query that her oversensitized mind had turned upside down. "In fact, I figured I could listen to these on my headphones while I clean. I'll have to go back through them later to do the indexes, of course, but it's anybody's guess when I'll have time for that.''

She wasted just a moment in regret. Coming back to Elmwood had seemed so straightforward at first, so simple. She'd just take a few months off from school to help out till Harry regained his strength, and at the same time she could do some serious work for her doctoral dissertation on the pioneer history of the area. But the time—to say nothing of the complications—just seemed to multiply. It was impossible to tell how long it would be before Harry was back in top form. And then there was the Merry Widow....

Danielle sighed. ''At least in the meantime I can check the quality of the recordings and see if the interviewers did a good job.''

''We've had more people interested in volunteering. But I'll put 'em off till you're finished with the Merry Widow.''

''Sometimes I wonder if I'll ever be finished with it,'' Danielle admitted.

It was the first time she'd actually allowed herself to think about the long term. What *would* they do if the Jablonskis didn't come back and no other sale materialized? Or, more to the point—because there was no question as to where Deke stood—what would *she* do?

Going to the museum to pick up the oral histories had been a stroke of genius. As Danielle cleaned, she listened to the older people of Elmwood, their recollections taped by volunteers who now and then asked a leading question. Without a doubt, she thought, this was the best batch yet. Her interviewers were getting better with each conversation, and the nuggets she could glean from these tapes would make a sparkling addition to her dissertation.

If she ever got around to writing it—which, at moments like this, looked increasingly unlikely.

It was midafternoon, the guests might be returning at any

time, and she still had one bedroom, one bath and the entire main floor public area to clean—plus she was due at the Willows in less than two hours to start greeting dinner guests.

Kate Jablonski had managed the whole job by herself. "And it would be no wonder if she was snappy sometimes because of it," Danielle muttered. But Kate hadn't had another job.

Danielle popped the tape of a retired barber, reminiscing about hairstyles and prices, from the tape player clipped to her belt and reached for the next one from the stack. A woman's voice, clipped and precise, brought tears to her eyes even before she consciously identified the speaker. Annabelle Fischer, talking to Danielle herself—the first oral history interview she'd conducted, when she'd been trying out the idea to see if it would work for her thesis.

Grief and longing swept over Danielle. Miss Fischer had been old and she'd said she was ready to die—but Danielle hadn't been ready to let her go. Until those last few months, Miss Fischer had always been the prim, proper English teacher whose standards for her students at Elmwood High had always seemed impossibly lofty…to the students at least. But at the end, Danielle had been allowed to see the woman underneath—the one who'd been a belle as a girl, the beloved darling of her wealthy father. The one who, as a very new teacher, had hidden her sense of humor under the cloak of dignity in order to maintain discipline among students who were barely younger than she was. The one who'd held her head high through the years even as her material fortunes declined.…

Danielle blotted the tears and put the tape safely in her handbag up in the Jablonskis' suite. She was on her way down the attic stairs when the front doorbell rang, and she was breathless by the time she reached it.

"Sorry," Pam said. "The way you're panting, I've either

dragged you away from something very interesting or very far away. Shall I take a stab at guessing which?''

"Very far away," Danielle said. "You can get yourself a glass of lemonade in the kitchen and follow me around while I clean, Pam, but—''

"Lemonade sounds good. I'll put this in the refrigerator while I'm there.'' Pam held up what looked like a tightly braided loaf of doughy white bread. "The instructions are on a card inside the bag. It'll rise in the refrigerator overnight, and in the morning you'll have cream cheese pastries for breakfast.''

"You're a love.'' Danielle gave her an impulsive hug. "I'll be in the front bedroom, right above the foyer.''

When Pam caught up with her a few minutes later, she carried two glasses of lemonade. "Take a break,'' she ordered. "I'll pitch in and help for an hour, till I have to pick Josh up at softball practice.''

The tears started again, blurring Danielle's vision. "You don't need to.''

"Hey, cleaning comes second nature to me. I have kids. Besides, after digging out at home, this kind of cleaning is fun. Sort of like the difference between washing the dishes every day and doing up the pretty party things.''

Danielle sat down on an overstuffed hassock beside the fireplace. "I'm so bogged down, Pam. What am I going to do? I've only been at this three days and already I'm in a hole so deep I can't see the top.''

"You'll get used to it. To juggling things, I mean, and working out a system so you can work faster.''

"I don't want to get used to it. I want a nice, quiet little ivory tower somewhere, with classes to teach and students to mentor and research to do. Running a bed-and-breakfast may sound like a glorious, relaxing profession, but it isn't my idea of how to spend my life.''

"You have to admit, Danny, it's hardly been a fair week

for a trial. Having this responsibility land on you with no warning, on top of your regular job... It must feel like being thrown into a swimming pool wearing a sequined ball gown.''

''And I'm dripping all over everything,'' Danielle agreed wryly. She drained her lemonade glass and set it aside. ''That helped—and I mean the reassurance as much as the drink. Maybe I *will* make it.''

From the doorway, Deke spoke. ''Oh, there you are, Danielle. Hi, Pam.''

Danielle was abruptly aware that she'd caught her hair up with a bandanna, that her blouse carried a dozen smears of dust and that she smelled like furniture polish and glass cleaner. Deke, on the other hand, was as immaculate as always. He'd left off jacket and tie, but his shirt was as crisp and blindingly white as if it had come from the store that morning, and the trimly tailored trousers didn't show a wrinkle.

''I have something for you to look at,'' he said, and only then did Danielle see the folder under his arm. ''A little organization seemed like a good idea.''

She took the folder almost warily, and the instant she opened it she knew why she'd felt that surge of trepidation. *A little organization* indeed! Fine type marched down the page in a neat outline, complete with headings and sub-headings, Roman numerals and capital letters—like soldiers marshaled into ranks for a full-dress parade.

He'd listed, step by step, all the jobs necessary to keep the Merry Widow running, divided room by room, area by area, day by day, week by week. It must have taken hours to think it all up and organize it so precisely.

Danielle closed the folder and threw it at him.

Less stable and airworthy than a paper airplane, the folder grabbed at the air and fluttered weakly to the floor, while each page sailed off separately.

Deke stooped to pick up the mess. "You aren't interested in my help?"

"If you want to help," Danielle said coldly, "how about doing something practical—like sweeping up the coffee cake crumbs from under the dining-room table. That would be helpful. *This*—" she jabbed a finger at the folder "—making lists of what I should do, and no doubt following me around telling me when I've done it badly and in the wrong order, is *not* helpful. So if you'll just get the hell out and let me do my job, Oliver..."

Her voice gave out.

Deke straightened the pages in the folder, laid it precisely on the corner of the bed and walked out.

Pam let her breath out in a long whistle.

"Can you *believe* the—the nerve?" Danielle sputtered.

"I've seen some in my day, but..." Pam reached for the folder.

Danielle drew back her foot, kicked the vacuum cleaner, then sank into the nearest chair, groaning.

"I think you ought to look at this, Danielle."

Pam's tone and the use of Danielle's full name made her sit up straight. "What? I saw all the neat little letters and numbers. What else...?"

Pam slid the last sheet out of the folder and handed it over. "It's not a checklist for you, Danny. It's for a hired cleaning person. Look here—on the back page there's a summary, and then it says 'Send applications to Box 72.'"

If Danielle's body had suddenly turned liquid, she couldn't have sunk farther into the overstuffed chair. She flung her head back and stared at the ceiling.

Great, she thought. *He tries to help, and you kick him out. Terrific move, Evans. Worthy of the world's great diplomats.*

Now all she could do was apologize.

At least, she thought grimly, she'd have to try. Whether Deke would be in any mood to listen was another matter altogether.

CHAPTER FIVE

DANIELLE made a mad dash for the stairs and plunged down to the main level, but she knew as she ran that she was too late. After the stinging lecture she'd handed him, Deke would have had no reason to stay around even for the couple of minutes that had passed. Still, she checked all the doors; his car wasn't under the porte cochere, and though from the front porch she could see almost to the square, she couldn't get a glimpse of him. While from the back door...

When she opened the back door, a man was standing on the porch just inches from her, fist raised to knock. Danielle wasn't sure which of them was the more surprised. She tried to look around him toward the carriage house, but his bulk made that difficult. She gave up what was surely a hopeless quest to catch up with Deke and said, "Is there something I can do for you?"

The man grinned. "I'd say it's the other way around, lady. I've got a delivery for you."

Danielle tried to smother a groan. "I'm sorry, but if it's something the Jablonskis ordered, I'm really not authorized to accept anything for them."

The man took his cap off and scratched behind his ear. "Look, lady, I don't know anything about the Jab-whatevers. My orders say I'm to deliver one premium-line portable dishwasher to the Merry Widow and charge it to Deke Oliver. Beyond that, I don't know nothing."

How about pouring salt in the wound? Danielle thought. If Deke had planned it, he couldn't have come up with more perfect timing.

She stepped back and waved a hand toward the kitchen. "Help yourself. Where do I sign?"

The dishwasher slid neatly into a corner of the kitchen. It had been an extremely thoughtful choice, Danielle realized. The portable would be less convenient to use since it had to be pulled over to the sink and hooked up each time, but it was functional from the instant it was uncrated. A built-in model would have called for total reconstruction of the area around the sink and a corresponding delay.

"Of course, you can hook it up permanently later," the delivery man said, "when you decide how you want the kitchen to look." He glanced around the room. "It's got all kinds of possibilities, doesn't it?"

"If that's a tactful way to say it's horribly old-fashioned and the best way to improve it would be dynamite, you're right."

The man grinned. "Well, at least you don't have to put those pretty hands in dishwater anymore. Just call us when you're ready for the final install."

Bemused, Danielle saw him to the door and walked back into the kitchen to load the dishes she'd left soaking in the sink. Except there weren't any. They'd been washed, dried and put away. For the first time, she remembered that she hadn't washed the ones the Jablonskis had left, either. Deke must have.

What was the matter with her anyway that she hadn't noticed before? And he'd spent his evenings at the Merry Widow when she couldn't be there....

"That was pure self-interest," she reminded herself. "Both to protect his investment and to get a little amusement from annoying me."

But the fact remained; while Deke's help hadn't fit the standard pattern, he'd been helping out all along. And she'd rewarded him with a temper tantrum.

She moaned and slapped both palms against her temples. This apology was not going to be fun.

By the end of the evening, Danielle was beginning to think that telling Deke she was sorry was going to be not just emotionally difficult but physically impossible. Every few minutes, when she could steal a bit of time from the customers waiting in the lobby of the Willows, she tried to phone him, alternating between his apartment and the Merry Widow. But all she got at either place was an answering machine. Even her guests must have all gone out for the evening; Danielle couldn't imagine three kids, one of them a teenager, ignoring a ringing telephone.

She finally gave up. Even if he was trying to stay out of her way, Deke couldn't avoid her altogether—not in a town the size of Elmwood. Sooner or later, she'd run into him.

The cold wind felt more like March than May when she left the Willows, and even the glow from the full moon was chilly rather than comforting. The Merry Widow looked only slightly warmer; there were lights on inside the house, but as Danielle climbed the stairs to the back porch, a cloud scudded across the moon and the sudden darkness almost made her miss her step.

The house was quiet; though she could hear the far-off rumble of a boom box, the sound was so faint that she couldn't identify the music or even tell which room it was coming from. The parlor and music room and hallway were quiet and dim, with only the flicker of moonlight and the soft glow of night-lights to show her the way to the main stairs.

The guests' doors were closed; from the front bedroom a long, contented, masculine snore sounded. Mr. Winslow was having a good night's sleep, Danielle concluded.

The rumble had grown more distinct as she climbed; now it died away and a moment later was replaced by the faint, mournful wail of a violin. The sound was coming from the top of the attic stairs, from inside the Jablonskis' suite.

She squared her shoulders and climbed the steps.

To one side of the staircase, almost in the center of the attic space, Kate Jablonski had spread an area rug to define a sort of sitting room. There, in an overstuffed chair with his back to the stairs, sat Deke.

It was foolish to feel relieved, Danielle told herself. A woman with sense would be disappointed right now that it wasn't Joe Jablonski sitting there, back at the Merry Widow to take up his duties. But undoubtedly her subconscious had considered that possibility and dismissed it before her foot even touched the bottom stair. Joe had never seemed the sort whose musical tastes ran to sophisticated string instruments.

No, she'd known it must be Deke. And her relief sprang from the fact that now she wouldn't have to go searching for him or take the chance of having to make her apology in some public place with an audience. Of course she was relieved about that; she wasn't a fool.

She certainly wasn't glad to see him for any other reason.

Danielle knew he'd heard her, for he turned his head a fraction and started to stand up.

She circled his chair. "I'm disappointed. Only a CD? I thought surely you'd be the one playing the violin, Deke." She waved him back, sat down in the chair that matched his and looked thoughtfully across at him. "I should have known—it sounded like a party up here. More noise than you could make by yourself."

"Really? I thought I was very restrained, considering I was more in the mood for a trumpet concerto."

Loud and violent, Danielle deduced. "I tried to call you earlier, to apologize."

"I was out."

"I noticed that. How is Norah these days?"

"Fine, I suppose. Any particular reason you're asking?"

"Because I can smell her perfume from here. And don't get the notion that I'm sniffing on purpose. A skunk with a head cold wouldn't have any trouble catching that aroma, the way she splashes it on. What's she doing—investing her divorce settlement in installments so she can keep you dropping by regularly?"

"You were, I believe, saying something about apologizing?"

Danielle bit her tongue. Why was she wasting time being catty anyway? "That's why I was trying to call you, yes."

Deke reached for the remote control lying on the table beside his chair and turned the CD's volume down even further. "There. Now you can go ahead. I wouldn't want to miss a word."

Danielle felt like sticking out her tongue, but no matter how he acted, her apology was every bit as necessary. "I'm sorry I jumped to conclusions about the duties list you made."

"I didn't create the list, actually. My housekeeper did."

"Well, that does explain how you knew what to put on it."

Deke raised one eyebrow.

Danielle winced. The words had been spoken before she'd stopped to think. "I didn't mean that the way it came out, exactly."

"Oh? What a relief."

Danielle decided the wisest course was to ignore the tinge of irony in his voice. "It was very kind of you to think of it, and of her to make the list."

"I'll pass along the gratitude, but Mrs. Baker was happy to help after I told her you had your hands full and didn't need another job right now. But she was very concerned about whether she'd anticipated everything that should go on the list, so she insisted I bring it over for you to approve.''

Danielle propped her elbow on the arm of her chair, leaned her face against her upraised hand and stared at him. ''You really like to go for the knockout, don't you? If you're trying to make me feel like a worm—''

''Oh, no,'' he said gently. ''I'd say you accomplished that all by yourself.''

''You've succeeded. I'll write your Mrs. Baker a note, okay? And while we're on the general subject of helpfulness, thanks for thinking of the dishwasher, too.''

''That,'' Deke said, ''was purely self-defense.'' He rose. ''If you're finished with your gracious repentance, Danielle—''

''I might as well be,'' Danielle said acidly, ''since even if I groveled it wouldn't make a difference.''

Deke's sudden smile lit up his face like sunrise on a still lake. ''I don't know about that. If you're convincing enough…''

The offer hung in the air for what seemed forever.

Danielle's heart was thudding in a slow, almost painful rhythm. ''Don't let me keep you,'' she said. To her own ears, her voice sounded as if she was at the bottom of a well.

Deke took two steps toward her and bent over her chair. His hand slid through the silky strands of her hair to cup the back of her head, and the cool touch of his fingers sent shards of ice racing down her spine.

He leaned closer till his lips were nearly touching hers. Danielle knew she should pull back, but she didn't seem to have enough control over her muscles to move at all. Suddenly, she couldn't smell Norah's perfume at all anymore, only Deke himself—warm and sultry and exciting.

Deke whispered, ''If you're convincing enough, I might even lend you Mrs. Baker.''

His mouth brushed hers so briefly, so softly, that she might have imagined it. But her reaction was far from imaginary; every cell in her body leaped to attention like individual soldiers on parade.

An instant later, Deke let her go and moved easily down the attic stairs, too quietly to disturb the sleeping guests. Danielle's ears, however, were sensitive enough to hear every step he took. Unless it was the blood pounding in her ears that she was hearing?

He was certainly in no hurry. *He's giving me a chance to think it over and call him back*, Danielle deduced.

Well, he'd be waiting a long, long time.

If you're convincing enough...

She was dead sure his definition had nothing to do with groveling.

Pam's party was in full swing by the time Danielle arrived at the Lannings' town house on Sunday afternoon, carrying a cheesecake and a bottle of wine. "Sorry I'm so late," she said as Pam greeted her with a hug.

"I saw the parking lot earlier. Brunch must have been crazy."

Danielle rolled her eyes. "It was—everybody in town must have visitors for the holiday weekend. But that's not why I was tied up. I just now got the last of our guests out of the Merry Widow and on the road. Why don't people seem to understand that checkout time applies in bed-and-breakfast places just as much as in regular hotels?"

"Charge them for an extra day just like the hotels do and they'll get the message soon enough," Pam advised.

"Careful, Pam, or people will think that old story's true, the one about accountants having ice water running in their veins."

"Just because I'm hardheaded? That's not from being an accountant. It's because I'm a mother."

"Well, I think even you would find extra charges easier to talk about than to impose."

Pam shook her head. "Why feel guilty about it? Warn them, of course. But it's only fair, especially when they're keeping other people from checking in."

"That was part of the problem, you see. There are no new guests till tomorrow—which ought to bother me since no guests means no money coming in. But after three days of constant fuss, the idea of a night off from the Merry Widow makes me feel like doing handsprings."

Pam feigned horror. "Not here, Danny, please! There's not enough room, and if you start, all the kids will want to join in!"

The Lannings' town house was indeed almost wall-to-wall people, from the front door past the dining table loaded with snacks and on to the sliding doors leading out to the patio. That was no surprise, Danielle thought. Pam threw some of the best parties in town, so it was no wonder that everyone who was invited had shown up.

Pam stood on tiptoe, trying to look over the crowd, and summoned her husband. "Greg, come here and relieve Danny of this food."

Danielle traded the cheesecake and wine for the chilled glass Greg Lanning offered. "You're a love, Greg." She took a sip and raised an eyebrow at Pam. "Strawberry punch? Aren't we getting a little ahead of ourselves?"

"I thought I should try out the recipe before the festival starts."

"Oh, that's right. I'd forgotten you volunteered to run the historical society's tea tent."

"'Volunteered' is not quite the word I'd choose. It was more like being drafted. Come over and get some hors d'oeuvres, Danny, before they're all gone." Pam plunged into the press of people and led the way. "This crowd is like starving locusts, and Greg just got the grill going half an hour ago, so it'll be a while before the rest of the food's ready.''

"I thought all your parties had to be over by eight in the evening or the neighbors started to object.''

"Oh, they still make a fuss, but I've learned how to handle the problem. I invited them, too." Pam's smile made her look particularly elfin. "One couple declined because they'd be out of town. I doubt they are, really—but now they can't possibly complain about the noise without giving themselves away.''

"You're a genius." Danielle looked out across the Lannings' minuscule deck and pocket-size backyard, separated from its neighbors by a split-cedar fence. On the far side of the fence, on a deck just as tiny, an elderly couple sat and glared at the Lannings' guests. "I see they refused the invitation, too. Pam, do you ever get an overwhelming urge to stand in the middle of your lawn and scream?''

"Just to annoy the neighbors, you mean? Oh, no—but I do get the urge to put up a twelve-foot brick wall. At least then I could pretend to have some privacy. But there are advantages to living here. For one thing, it's cheap—relatively speaking, that is—so I don't have to work full-time.''

"And you can pamper the clients you do take on, for which we are humbly grateful.''

"Well, I doubt a full-time boss would see the necessity of stopping by a client's business every day," Pam admitted.

"Much less two or three times a day." Danielle was thinking about the Willows. "I know how much of a load it takes off Dad and me, not having to fuss with the records or the banking.''

"And I can be home with my kids more, for which they are *not* grateful in the least." Pam raised her voice. "Josh, stop tormenting the cat!''

The president of the historical society, obviously no

worse for wear because of being stranded in the museum's window the day before, tapped Pam on the shoulder. "Not bad," she said, holding up a fresh glass of punch. "But if next time you added a little rum—"

"No, Martha," Pam said firmly. "You know what the society's trustees said about serving alcohol at the strawberry festival."

Martha grinned. "They're just a bunch of old fogies," she confided. "Not a new idea among them. Not that spiking the punch would be a new idea, of course, since that little trick must have been thought of within fifteen minutes after the discovery of fermentation. But as long as we're on the subject of new ideas and discoveries…"

Danielle reached for a stuffed mushroom cap. "What historic treasure are you tracking down now?"

Martha shook her head. "Haven't heard of anything good lately, which must mean the museum's due for a windfall. No, this is completely different. You know the money that's been donated lately?"

Danielle popped the mushroom into her mouth and reached for another one. "Did you decide to hire some help after all?"

"Oh, no. But I got to thinking a few weeks back that it was just sitting in the bank not earning much, and it seemed to me we could do a lot better if we got into the stock market or those what-you-call-'ems. Virtual funds."

Foreboding as dark as a summer thunderstorm made Danielle's fingers close tightly on her mushroom, squeezing the savory filling out into her hand. Surely, she thought, Martha hadn't taken some kind of crazy flyer in the market. No, she couldn't have; Martha might talk, but she had far too much sense to actually take that kind of risk. Danielle breathed a little more easily and even managed a smile as she reached for a napkin to wipe cheese off her fingers. "I think you mean mutual funds."

"Well, whatever they're called, they sure pay better than the bank does."

"Some of them do. But they can be risky—you can lose big, too. So unless you know what you're doing..."

"I never said I knew one from another." Martha sounded almost insulted at the idea. "But I found some-body who does, and he took over the whole problem. Told me not to worry a bit—and he was right. I just got the first results today, and guess what! In just over a month, he practically doubled our money."

Danielle choked on her mushroom. This wasn't possible, she told herself frantically. The staid old-school members of the trustees' committee would never have approved of a flyer crazy enough to earn a hundred percent interest in thirty days. "The trustees..." she managed to say. Then certainty settled like a lump of lead in her stomach. "You didn't even consult the trustees, did you?"

Martha grinned and snapped her fingers. "By golly, *that's* what I forgot to do! Guess I'll have to tell them at next month's meeting and apologize all over myself."

Danielle glanced at Pam, who looked stunned. Join the crowd, Danielle thought. "And you're telling us," she ventured, "in the hope that we'll convince the trustees you did the right thing?"

"Oh, I wouldn't turn down the help if you feel like lob-bying them. But that's not why I'm talking about it—I'm just so pleased I had to tell somebody. Besides, I imagine, considering the outcome, even that stick-in-the-mud bunch will give the go-ahead to reinvest it all. And that'll be a mighty good thing," Martha confided with a sly smile, "since I already have."

"Martha." Danielle put both hands on the woman's shoulders and looked straight into her eyes. "Listen to me. Get out of this scheme while you still have the money. You might as well be betting on a slot machine as investing in something you don't know about.''

"I'm not," Martha said patiently. "Deke is."

Of course it would be Deke. But even though Danielle had been expecting it, the name still fell on her like acid rain.

"Such a nice young man, isn't he?" Martha said gently. "And he knows so much about money. I still don't understand why you turned him down, Danielle."

Danielle took a deep breath. "And just how do you think Deke makes *his* money?"

"Oh, he explained all that to me. He gets a percentage of what the client earns. So if he makes more money for the client, he benefits, too, and everybody's happy."

"Or if he can pull a little sleight of hand and make it look like a better return," Danielle said grimly, "the client reinvests and Deke earns twice as much. I'd really like to know what in *hell* he invested in that's supposedly making such an obscene amount of interest."

"I don't think he told me." Martha's voice was tranquil. "Or if he did, I don't remember. But Deke's right here, so you can ask him."

Danielle spun around so fast she almost lost her balance.

Deke was no more than two steps from her, with a wide-eyed Norah close beside him. Perhaps, Danielle thought, the woman was encountering a few sudden doubts about the wisdom of her own investments?

Deke was smiling, but there wasn't much humor in his voice. "Perhaps Danielle would like to take over the job," he suggested mildly. "I'll happily step aside in that case. But I couldn't square it with my conscience, Martha, not to urge caution if Danielle suggests you invest in the Merry Widow."

Fury rose as bitter as bile in Danielle's throat. "Dammit, Deke, just because I wanted to save the house instead of seeing it wrecked is no reason to blame the whole mess on me. Money was never the object—''

''Of course it wasn't,'' Deke murmured.

Danielle's face flamed as she remembered exactly what Deke thought *had* been in her mind at the time. She bit her lip and tried to will the hot blood away. ''And it wasn't my idea to get the Merry Widow thrown back at us, either. But this whole discussion really has nothing to do with the Merry Widow.''

''I wondered if you'd notice that.''

Danielle glared at him. ''So can we just go back to discussing the museum?''

''Of course. But perhaps first you'll tell me why you're taking such a personal interest, Danielle. As I recall, you aren't even a member of the board of trustees. Or have I missed a development lately?''

Danielle swallowed hard. She'd almost forgotten, in the heat of the moment, that the last thing she wanted was to give Deke—or anyone else for that matter—reason to question why she felt so strongly about the issue. He was right; she didn't have any official standing where the museum was concerned.

In fact, Danielle reminded herself, she had no real right to an opinion at all. That money had ceased to be hers the moment she'd wrapped up and dispatched the first bundle of cash. It belonged to the museum now—to use or to lose—and she had nothing more to say about it.

She gritted her teeth. ''I merely want to know what you invested in that brings such fantastic rewards. Antique dolls? Baseball cards? Maybe a newly discovered gold mine?''

''Surely you wouldn't expect me to give away my professional methods in public, would you, darling?'' His voice was low and intimate, though Danielle knew it carried precisely as far as Deke wanted it to. "But if what you really want is to join in the fun…"

He raised a hand to her face, pushing her hair back so he could toy with her earlobe. In the press of people, Danielle couldn't even move away. But the crowd wouldn't notice that, she knew. They'd see only that the gesture looked like the easy familiarity of a lover. Norah certainly didn't miss the nuances; her eyes narrowed, and Danielle could almost feel the venom in her stare.

Deke's voice dropped another notch. "Just let me know, and I'll happily whisper all my secrets right into your little ear." He released her hair, letting it spill forward once more.

Norah murmured something to him, and he offered an arm to her. She took it, casting a triumphant look at Danielle, and the two of them moved off toward the patio.

Danielle absently rubbed the back of her neck, where the muscles felt like tightly strung cables. "Martha," she began once more, but the woman had drained her glass while Danielle wasn't looking and strolled across to the punch bowl.

Pam shook her head. "It ought to be interesting to watch the fireworks when the trustees hear about this. There'll probably be a move to impeach Martha."

"Unless they grant her sainthood because of her financial abilities," Danielle said dryly. "I'll bet the trustees don't know much more about the financial markets than Martha does. You know, I can understand how she got caught up in this. She doesn't even know the right questions to ask. But for Deke to take advantage of her inexperience…"

That, Danielle realized, was really what was bothering her, even more than the fact that Deke had put the museum's money at tremendous risk—which he must have, in order to have scored such a quick, immense gain. The idea that he hadn't warned Martha, made sure she understood the chances she was taking, both by investing so wildly and by doing so without the approval of the museum's trustees...

Fancy that, Danielle jeered at herself. *Despite everything, I still cherish some illusions about him.*

Or, more accurately, she *had*. Now all that was left was an empty feeling in the pit of her stomach.

She stood there for a full minute longer, staring unseeingly at the snack table and trying to decide if she should simply declare exhaustion and go home. She was bone tired, true—but would that make Deke think he'd won the round? And why should she give a moment's consideration to what he might think?

When Kevin came up beside her and slipped an arm around her shoulders, Danielle jumped six inches.

"Sorry," he said. "When did you come in? I thought I'd kept one eye on the door for better than an hour, but all of a sudden I look up and you're not only here, you're turning Deke Oliver into sausage."

Danielle laughed, then realized that there was no irony in his voice. "It's sweet of you to feed my ego, Kevin," she said, "but I really don't think I was the winner in that round."

"No? You looked pretty good to me. And he's the one who backed off and went slinking away with that fake blonde. What's the deal with her anyway? She's new, isn't she?"

"Not really. Norah grew up here, went away, got married, got divorced, came home to heal with the help—so they say—of a substantial settlement."

"Oh, *that's* why he's interested." Kevin's fingers kneaded her shoulder, and Danielle's tense muscles started to relax. "Come on, Greg just said the hamburgers are ready. Let me feed the rest of you, not just your ego."

Danielle hesitated. But Kevin's face held nothing but

friendliness, and his touch was neither demanding nor possessive, just soothing. Obviously, she thought with relief, somewhere along the line he'd finally gotten the message that while she was delighted to be his friend, she could never look at him as anything more.

Still, caution made her ask, "Just a hamburger, right? Nothing more?"

Kevin's brows drew together, and her heart sank. "Well, maybe a pickle, too," he said. "And some macaroni salad. Would that be going too far?"

She saw a teasing sparkle in his eyes and laughed. What a joy it would be to simply have fun—tease, talk, dance and enjoy her friends—without worrying about anything. Not Kevin…and certainly not Deke.

Her decision to stay and have a good time had nothing to do with Deke. She wasn't trying to prove anything to him.

And a good thing it was, too, she thought, as she followed Kevin out onto the deck and saw Deke standing on the far side of the lawn with Norah still clinging to his arm.

Because Deke probably wouldn't even notice.

CHAPTER SIX

THE bungalow was almost dark when Danielle tiptoed in. After just a few nights away, she felt almost like a stranger, even though she'd grown up in the house. Partly, she supposed, that was because she'd stopped thinking of it as home in the time she'd been away, and though she'd been back in Elmwood for a year now, she still thought of the move as temporary. Till Harry was well enough that he didn't need her anymore and she could go back to school— the words had almost become a mantra.

She was setting her foot on the first step when Harry's gruff voice stopped her. "Reminds me of the old days," he said, "when you were a bit late for curfew and trying to sneak past your mother."

Danielle retraced her steps to the arched doorway between the living room and hallway. She'd passed it, thinking the room was empty, because he'd been sitting at his desk in the far corner, almost in the dark because his body had blocked the thin stream of light from the goosenecked lamp. He was wearing his glasses low on his nose, and a blizzard of paper lay across the blotter.

Danielle leaned over his shoulder and kissed his cheek. "And you'd help me get away with it," she accused lightly. "Surely you haven't forgotten that part?"

Harry didn't smile. "I miss her, Danny."

The low, wistful note in his voice brought a lump to Danielle's throat. It had been almost ten years since her mother died. Though Harry seldom mentioned her, Danielle knew that his wife was never far from his thoughts. She would have expected nothing less; the two of them had been a team all through the years of building the Willows from a casual café to a first-class restaurant.

She laid her cheek against Harry's soft pink bald spot, and her arms tightened around his shoulders. "Me, too."

Harry turned his head and smiled up at her with obvious effort. "How was the party?"

"Like most of Pam's. Hectic, noisy and lots of fun."

"Was somebody outside with you just now?"

"No. Why?"

"I was sure I heard another car. Thought maybe you'd brought someone home."

"Like who?" Danielle's voice was dry. "Kevin, and give him all kinds of ideas again?"

As a matter of fact, Kevin had wanted to bring her home, and though he'd acted like the perfect friend all evening, Danielle had been glad of the excuse that she didn't need a ride because she had her own car. Enjoying herself with him at the party was one thing; there hadn't been anything exclusive about it, and she'd had the same kind of fun with a lot of other people. So had Kevin, she thought. But letting him bring her home would have made it seem just a little too much like a date.

Harry pushed his glasses higher on his nose. "Elmwood's not very exciting for you anymore, is it?"

"It's fine, Dad."

"I'm sorry, my dear."

"For what? Getting sick? Don't be silly."

Harry nodded. "And for the fact that you couldn't finish school."

"*Didn't*," Danielle corrected. "Not *couldn't*. And with the correspondence courses I've been taking, I really haven't lost all that much anyway."

"Yes, you keep telling me you can catch up whenever you get back. But..."

A note of laughter crept into Danielle's voice. "It's not

as if history won't be the same when I get back to it, Dad.
It's not like computers or medicine. And if I don't get my
Ph.D. till I'm forty, what difference does it make? Family's
more important.'' In the reflection of yellow light cast by
the goosenecked lamp, she could see the glimmer of tears
in Harry's eyes, and she hastily looked for another subject
before his sentimentality overwhelmed and embarrassed
him. ''Daddy, have you ever heard much about Deke's
business? How it's going, his ethics—that sort of thing?''

Harry considered. ''Heard a couple of guys say they'd
lost some money in the stock market after they'd gotten a
tip from Deke.''

Danielle frowned. ''I suppose nobody can promise every
investment will do well, but—''

''I think it's more likely he was only chatting and they
just thought they got a hot tip. But that's the only thing
I've ever heard against him. He doesn't seem to have a lot
of clients—or else they're very quiet about it. He certainly
looks successful. New car every year, and everybody seems
to like him.''

But what does anybody really know about him? Danielle
wanted to ask. Even she had never noticed how little Deke
said about himself. She knew he was the child of long divorced parents and that he'd grown up on the East Coast—
but she couldn't remember any specifics or even exactly
how she knew. It certainly hadn't been during some heart-
to-heart discussion.

But she thought she'd already said too much. The orig-
inal question had been pointless anyway; if there had ever
been a whisper about Deke's ethics, all of Elmwood would
know it. Which didn't mean he was absolutely pure, of
course. As long as people like Martha continued to be
lucky, they'd be absolutely satisfied. And even if their luck
ran out, they wouldn't necessarily blame Deke—and so

there'd be no reason to question whether he'd benefit even from their loss.

A hundred percent interest in thirty days, Danielle mused. She doubted he was investing his own money at that rate because of the risk that must be part of the package. And a shame it was, too—because if he was pulling in that kind of return, she wouldn't feel nearly so bad about not having her half of the cash to repair the Merry Widow's roof!

She dropped a kiss on Harry's bald spot and went upstairs to her room.

On the same small table where she'd done her grade-school homework were a couple of textbooks and a single big white envelope that Harry must have put there since she'd been home last—an envelope she knew would contain the latest set of problems she'd completed for her statistical analysis class, returned with a grade and the next assignment in the series.

Despite what she'd told Harry, she was not keeping up with her studies. The correspondence courses were helping, but the glacial pace was frustrating; she'd completed only a few credits, and few of the classes she needed were available that way.

But there was no point in feeling sorry for herself. Everything else she'd said to her father had been correct— family *was* more important, and her studies would be waiting no matter when she got back to them. There might even be an advantage to being older when she started seeking her first job on a college faculty, she thought whimsically. If she had gray hair, she'd probably stand out from the rest of the first-time applicants!

And right now, she reminded herself, the fact that she didn't have firm deadlines for papers and set dates for exams was a blessing. She'd worry about how to handle the

rest of her schooling when the strawberry festival was over
and when the Merry Widow was sold.

If that day ever came.

The answering machine in the music-room-turned-office
was blinking furiously when Danielle came down from settling Monday's single guest, a fiftyish businessman, into
the Merry Widow's best bedroom. It had been twenty-four
hours since she'd left the house, but she wasn't prepared
for the telephone to have gone wild in her absence.

"What did everybody do?" she groaned. "Wait on purpose for the one night I wasn't here, then all call at once?"

She got the reservations book—a gesture she hoped
would be justified by the content of the calls—and settled
in to listen to the messages.

The first was an excited bride-to-be in a neighboring
town, looking for a place to have her wedding reception.
Danielle sighed. She'd have to call with regrets, of course;
the Merry Widow wasn't set up for such events. And a
shame it was, too, she thought. If Kate and Joe had gone
after business like that...

"I'd *really* be tearing my hair out about now," she muttered.

There were two wrong numbers, a couple of calls from
Danielle's friends and one genuine request for reservations.
The trouble was, Mrs. DeCarlo wanted two rooms right
smack in the middle of the strawberry festival—when
Danielle had nothing left to offer.

She dialed the number Mrs. DeCarlo had left, but all she
got was an endlessly ringing telephone. Par for the course,
she told herself. The Jablonskis' answering machine was
an economy model, so she couldn't tell precisely when the
woman had called. Danielle put the number on her list of
things to do and went on to the next message. It was Norah,

calling with a little laugh to see if Deke might be at the Merry Widow since he wasn't at home.

"And obviously he's not at her place, either," Danielle murmured, and found herself wondering what time of day that call had been made. Only, she assured herself, because it would help pinpoint when Mrs. DeCarlo had phoned and perhaps make it easier to catch her at home. She was definitely *not* interested in where Deke was spending his time.

By the time she'd finished with the last of the messages, the businessman had changed his clothes and gone out for the evening. Danielle realized just as his car pulled away that she'd forgotten to give him a key. If Deke was planning to come this evening, there wouldn't be a problem. But *was* he? After the squabble they'd had yesterday at Pam's party, Danielle was almost afraid to count on it and didn't particularly want to track him down to ask.

She called the Willows instead to tell her father she'd probably be running behind schedule.

"That's all right," Harry said. "Don't bother to come in. There are so few tables booked tonight that we'll all be standing around staring at each other anyway."

"Everybody must be staying home till the weekend, when the festival starts."

"And then they'll all be here at once, standing in line grumbling about why we don't have enough space," Harry agreed. "Get some rest, dear, and don't feel guilty. How long has it been since you took a day off?"

The evening stretched before her in unexpected glory. She needed to sort through the mail again; though she'd checked it every day to look for reservations, she'd simply opened, glanced at, then stacked the bills. After the weekend's crowd, there was a little money—but not enough to cover everything. Deciding which debts to pay first would be the problem. Should she pay a lot of little accounts or wipe out one big one completely? Or maybe scatter small payments around everywhere and hope that all the creditors would be appeased for a while?

But that wouldn't take long, and once it was done, the entire evening lay before her. Though there were no doubt a hundred things that needed doing, Danielle was in no mood to tackle any of them. She'd do something fun instead. How long *had* it been since she'd taken a day off from the Willows? And even today didn't entirely count, considering she'd worked the lunch hour.

She was stretched out in a maroon velvet chair in the front parlor, staring at the ceiling while she enumerated her options, when she heard Deke's footsteps in the hall. She sat up just as he paused in the doorway.

He looked a bit surprised to see her. "This is an unanticipated pleasure, Danielle. Let me guess. You told Harry you'd much rather run the Merry Widow full-time than be tied to the restaurant, so—"

"Please." Danielle shuddered. "I'd take the Willows a million times instead."

Deke pulled a straight-backed chair around and straddled it, folding his arms across the carved back. "I don't get it," he said.

"Preferring the Willows to the Merry Widow? Come on, Deke, you're the one who keeps saying this house is a curse, a hopeless cause, a financial drain of the same proportions as the national debt—"

"I'm absolutely certain I never compared the Merry Widow to the national debt."

"Well, maybe you weren't quite that specific, but you implied it."

"Because I think dollar for dollar, it's probably even worse. At least the nation has assets to balance off against the deficit. At any rate, my question had nothing to do with the Merry Widow. You'd have to be totally crazy to prefer the Merry Widow over anything else, especially after spending a few days in the business, and whatever else you are, Danielle, you're not a complete crackpot. I was asking—''

"Pardon me for my lack of enthusiasm about the compliment," she said. "If, that is, it was intended to be a compliment."

"Consider it however you like. I was asking why you're still at the Willows after all these months."

"Because my father needs me."

"Harry's as well as he's ever going to be."

The unemotional, straightforward announcement set Danielle's teeth on edge—largely, she admitted, because it was true, and because she didn't want to face the reality that Harry might never be in truly good health again. "Of course, if I'd gone back to Chicago after his first crisis was past," she pointed out, "I wouldn't have been here when the Jablonskis left to insist that we take over."

"That fact had occurred to me."

"Actually," Danielle added thoughtfully, "I wouldn't even have been here to give Miss Fischer nutty ideas."

"I'd also thought of that."

"And look how very dull your life would have been in consequence." Danielle shrugged. "You'd have had to get *all* your excitement from the stock market. Speaking of which, I'd still like to know how you pulled off the coup with the museum's money."

"The minute you get elected to the board of trustees, just let me know, and I'll happily fill you in. In the meantime, the museum's my client, Danielle. You're not."

"I'm just concerned, that's all. Martha has no business getting into something she doesn't understand."

Deke nodded. "That's why she called me."

"But..." Danielle took a deep breath and tried again. "She's not just a novice, Deke, she's a complete innocent. She doesn't have a clue that the museum could end up with nothing at all. She thinks you're some kind of magician where cash is concerned—''

''Perhaps you think you could do better?''

Annoyed, Danielle snapped, ''I couldn't do worse.''

Deke's eyebrows lifted slowly. His eyes narrowed and seemed to darken to cold steel.

''I'm not talking about interest rates,'' she said. ''I was talking about handling things conservatively. Martha might not get as large a return if I was in charge, but she wouldn't be likely to lose the whole works, either.''

''Oh, yes. The Danielle Evans school of investing. Tell me again what you did with all the money you've gotten from the Merry Widow so far? And why it seems to be doing you no good?''

Her heart jolted and then returned to its normal rhythm. She'd taken a jab at him and so he'd retaliated, striking at what he knew was a sensitive spot. But that didn't mean he'd discovered exactly why Danielle found it such a touchy subject.

He couldn't know, she reassured herself. Martha couldn't have told him because she was unaware herself of the source of the funds. And he couldn't have figured it out from the record of donations—which Martha probably hadn't given him anyway—because Danielle hadn't been foolish enough to give the museum the precise amount of the Jablonskis' payment each month. She'd rounded it off to a nice even number and hadn't even made the donations on a regular basis. Sometimes she cashed the Jablonskis' check right away; sometimes she waited a week or two before she dropped the bundle of money into the museum's mail slot. Sometimes she'd even skipped a month and later lumped two payments together.

She'd been very careful to leave no pattern, nothing that might lead suspicious minds back to her. And because of the irregularity of her donations, it would be six weeks at

least before Martha or the trustees realized that the donations had stopped—too long a span of time for anyone to
connect the break with the Jablonskis' defection.

No, Deke couldn't have figured it out. He was only trying to distract her thoughts from Martha's investment by
playing on Danielle's weaknesses. She was safe.

"Stop changing the subject," she recommended.
"You're obviously very good at your job—"

"Why do I suspect this is not really a pat on the back?"

"So why aren't you in demand in New York City?"

"Who said I'm not?" Deke asked gently.

"And you're still here despite it? Don't tell me the people on Wall Street couldn't find some incentives you'd find
tempting. The point is, hotshot investment people usually
don't hang around for long in places like Elmwood."

"Maybe I like things dull."

"You? Don't make me laugh. And why did you come
to Elmwood in the first place? You know, I can't believe I
never wondered about that before." *Talk about stupid questions*, Danielle told herself. *You were too fascinated with
the man himself to ponder his past or speculate whether he
might be hiding out from something.*

"Why Elmwood?" Deke shrugged. "Simple. I played
pin-the-tail-on-the-donkey with a map of the country."

She stared dubiously at him.

"What does it matter where I am?" Deke sounded exasperated. "In an era of fax machines, instant communi-
cation and computer networks, I don't need to even be in
the same state as my clients. And what could I do on Wall
Street that I can't do here?"

"Get run over by a bull or a bear?" Danielle asked hopefully. "Though, believe me, if you lose Martha's money,
you'd rather encounter a bull or a bear than her wrath. Trust
me, Deke—I know her. And I'm looking out for your best
interests."

"I'm touched that you're worried about me."

There was a husky catch in his voice that made Danielle feel very skeptical.

"You might even say I'm thankful," Deke went on.

"Knock it off, Oliver."

"In fact, your concern gives me a little ache, right here." He tapped the center of his chest, then looked very thoughtful. "Or maybe that's not gratitude at all. It might be hunger instead."

Danielle gave up. "I wouldn't expect you to know the difference. You probably can't tell an attack of conscience from a migraine, either. Well, don't say I didn't warn you. If that fund's performance falls flat next month, Martha will be screaming her horror even louder than she's singing your praises right now."

"You're hoping, aren't you? Well, give it enough time and we'll see who's right. I think, since you're here to man the fort, I'll run down to the restaurant on the square and pick up something for dinner. Shall I bring enough for two, or do you only eat food prepared in the kitchen of the Willows?"

"I'm not that much of a snob and I'd love a grilled tenderloin." Danielle added dryly, "Do you want me to pay you for the sandwich now or when you get back?"

"Oh, don't worry about it." Deke's voice was airy. "Since I've been skimming money from the museum's account all month, I've got plenty of cash to cover the bill for now. I'll just add it to what you owe me for the roof repairs."

He disappeared down the hall, and Danielle sank back into her chair. Why did merely talking to the man have to be so exhausting? It never used to be that way—but of course, in the days when they'd been dating, she hadn't felt the need to be constantly on guard.

Now, she felt nothing but on guard where Deke Oliver was concerned.

Nothing else at all.

She picked up a book one of the weekend guests had left on the parlor table, but she couldn't get interested in the story. In fact, she was almost asleep in her chair when the ringing of the doorbell jolted her upright. Deke? Surely not; he must have his key. The businessman, returning early? Maybe he'd only run an errand or two instead of going out to the Willows for dinner as she'd recommended.

But when she opened the door, she found Kevin on the porch instead. "I stopped at the Willows to see you," he said, "but your dad said you were taking the night off. So I thought I'd come keep you company."

Before she could find the gentle words it would take to discourage him without rudeness, Kevin had somehow crossed the threshold and was in the foyer, grinning down at her and so clearly pleased with himself that she didn't have the heart to throw him out. Besides, it wasn't as if she'd actually made other plans.

He held up a videocassette. "I even stopped to get a movie since you never seem to have time to go to the theater. I hope this one's okay—the guy at the rental place said women love it."

Danielle glanced at the title and smiled. "That's sweet, Kevin. I've wanted to see this. I even rented it once myself, but I never got around to watching it."

"My good luck," he said lightly. "Point me to the nearest television set."

"There's only one, and it's all the way upstairs in the Jablonskis' suite."

"Well, I don't suppose it'd look real fitting in the midst of all this old furniture."

"Hardly, to say nothing of the difficulties if the guests couldn't agree on what to watch. Much better to prevent the problem than to try to solve it after the fight starts. I'll get some soft drinks and meet you by the stairs.''

Kevin had gone on up when she came back with a couple of Cokes and a bag of chips she'd unearthed from the top of a cabinet. When Deke came back, she thought, she'd offer to share her tenderloin with Kevin. The way the restaurant on the square prepared them, the sandwiches were big enough for two.

He leaned over the stair rail and called, ''Nice place. I was never upstairs before. The rooms are bigger and lighter than I expected.''

Danielle swallowed her annoyance. It was hardly fair to be irritated at him for looking into the bedrooms when the doors stood open on all but the one that was rented tonight.

She led the way up the attic stairs. ''Brace yourself. This is neither big nor well lighted.''

Kevin stood at the top of the stairs and looked around. ''Oh, it's not so bad. In fact, I'll bet it's kind of exciting in a storm, with rain pounding on the roof and thunder all around.''

Danielle shivered. ''I haven't had the experience and I'm not looking forward to it.''

Kevin laughed and went to put the videotape in the machine. Danielle curled up on the couch and popped the top of her soft-drink can. Kevin sat down beside her just as she raised the can to take a drink, and the bouncing of the saggy springs sent Coke surging from the can over Danielle's face.

''Oh, damn,'' he said, and slid closer, pulling a handkerchief from his pocket. ''Here, look at me.'' He wiped her cheek and chin and then bent closer. His voice was unsteady. ''It's still sticky. Let me...''

Danielle tried to pull away, but his hand on her shoulder held her close. ''That's fine, Kevin. I—''

His kiss landed awkwardly, halfway between her mouth and chin.

Danielle leaned as far back as she could. "Kevin," she said firmly, "that's not why I invited you up here. I've told you before, I think of you as a friend—"

"That was before the party yesterday."

"Nothing happened at the party except that we had a good time—as friends."

"Yeah? Well, I've tried thinking of you as a friend, and it doesn't work, Danielle. I'm crazy about you." His arm tightened, drawing her closer, and his lips brushed the corner of her mouth. "It's more than that, it's got to be more than that. You have to feel it, too…"

The soft-drink can Danielle still held limited her mobility, while Kevin had the use of both hands. When he cupped one palm around her breast, Danielle coolly considered dumping the rest of her Coke down his back. Icy, fizzy, sticky liquid sluicing down his spine ought to bring him back to his senses, she hoped.

Just as she started to tip the can, a low voice only a couple of feet behind the couch said, "Excuse me, Kevin…but does the phrase 'You're trespassing' mean anything to you, buddy?" Deke leaned one hip against the back of the couch till he was half-sitting just behind Danielle, then he reached over to ruffle her hair.

The relief surging through her at the sound of his voice receded just as quickly. He could have stopped with "Excuse me", she thought irritably, and he would have accomplished the same thing. But no—Deke always had to take things to the edge.

"Maybe I like things dull," he'd told her less than an hour ago.

Yeah, right, she thought. *And the Merry Widow will sprout wings and fly, too.*

Kevin glared at her. ''You told me there was nothing to those rumors about you and him!''

This, Danielle told herself, was the best example she'd ever experienced of being caught between a rock and a hard place.

Before she could answer, Deke had stood up and was shepherding Kevin toward the stairs. ''Sorry you can't stay,'' he said coolly. ''And before you come back, you might reconsider how friends behave.''

A couple of minutes later, she heard the front door slam. When Deke reappeared, he was chuckling softly, and the fact that he found the whole thing funny sent flames of fury licking along Danielle's nerves. She faced him squarely. ''And what exactly did you mean by 'trespassing', Deke?''

''I thought he was going to start licking you any minute. Surely you aren't going to tell me that sort of manhandling isn't trespassing on your rights?''

''Oh, no. That wasn't the impression you left. You very clearly implied I'm your property.''

''Once upon a time,'' he said very softly, ''you wanted to be.''

''No, I didn't. You *thought* I wanted to be. You actually believe that no woman could possibly be in your company and not want to own you—or be owned. Well, I'm here to tell you, Deke Oliver...''

He rounded the end of the couch and sat down on the overstuffed arm. ''Even if Kevin took what I said to mean he was stomping on my rights instead of yours, what's the problem? It was effective, wasn't it? I don't think he'll be back.''

''That's beside the point. I didn't ask to be rescued, Deke. I didn't *need* to be rescued!''

His eyes widened. ''I suppose that means you actually wanted the puppy to stay? Oh, I am sorry, Danielle. Shall I go whistle for him?''

Danielle gritted her teeth. "You are deliberately... For once, would you just listen? *I do not need to be rescued.* I could've handled him. I've been dealing with drunks and other impossible people at the Willows since I was sixteen. For the last time, Deke Oliver, I can handle *anything*. Is that clear enough for you?"

Her words echoed from the high-peaked ceiling and slowly died away, leaving the murmur of the forgotten videotape as the only sound in the room.

The corner of Deke's mouth quirked slightly upward. He shifted his perch on the arm of the couch, stretching his feet out a bit farther as if to brace himself. "Really?" He reached out, almost casually, and his hand came to rest on her elbow. "Well, I'm not drunk, but I think you'd probably classify me as impossible. So show me how you do it, Danielle. Handle me."

One swift pull brought her next to him till she stood between his knees, her face precisely on a level with his. Except that she wasn't standing, precisely; she was leaning against him, her breasts firmly pressed against his chest. Her arms had gone around him in a futile effort to regain her lost balance.

His hand slid to the nape of her neck and drew her very slowly closer, till his mouth seared hers. Heat spread through her muscles; flame licked at every centimeter of her body. Her bones ached and then melted.

She didn't know how she ended up lying on the couch with Deke beside her. Had he eased her onto the cushions or had she pulled him down? She didn't care. Without the need to hold herself upright, Danielle was free to concentrate on the sensual feast he offered. The slight taste of salt on his skin. The scent of his aftershave. The tiny groan he uttered...or did that sound come from her throat instead?

Suddenly, while she still sprawled across the couch, Deke sat up and then pushed himself to his feet. He stood for a moment looking down at her and said dryly, "Great demonstration, Danielle. I see now how you handle these things. Maybe I should hunt the puppy down and give him some pointers."

And he walked away, leaving her there—so shaken that she thought she might never be able to stand up again, so confused that she didn't want to try.

CHAPTER SEVEN

DANIELLE flung her arm across her eyes as if by doing so she could refuse to see reality. But the effort was futile, for the facts were burned upon her brain and hiding wouldn't diminish the truth—that in the space of minutes, she'd made a fool of herself...twice.

The first mistake, making that stupid declaration about not needing to be rescued, had been bad enough. Why hadn't she just said a firm, chilly thank-you for Deke's timely interruption? Why had she felt it so important to drive home the point that she could take care of herself?

"Because you have the knack of asking for trouble," she chided herself. She might as well have stood in the middle of a stadium full of starving lions waving a slab of raw beef.

But it was the second bit of foolishness that truly haunted Danielle. Once having taken her stand, planted the flag and declared herself the queen of self-control, she should have stuck to her guns no matter what. But no—she'd promptly collapsed the instant Deke had challenged her. All he'd done, really, was pull her close and kiss her, and her boast had vanished in a puff of dust, leaving him free to do exactly as he pleased....

Heat flared through her body once more. She could feel his hands caressing her, his weight against her, the sensual rasp of his slightly stubbly cheek against hers. She could still taste him, and his aroma seemed to have soaked into her bones....

She should have known what would happen. If she'd given it even the most fleeting thought, she would have realized that Deke could no more have ignored that challenge than he could walk on the ceiling. She'd practically dared him—and the result had been as predictable as night following day.

But she hadn't seen it coming. Or…had she known it would happen and pushed the buttons anyway? Had she *wanted* to provoke him and simply got a little more than she'd bargained for?

The suspicion left a brassy taste on her tongue.

He'd always been able to kiss her halfway to oblivion without apparent effort. But the key word was *halfway*. Danielle had always known that no matter how much he'd enjoyed himself—and the catch in his voice and the speed of his breathing made it obvious that he liked kissing her very much indeed—there was a corner of Deke's mind that stood apart, as if watching with a cynical smile.

From the first time he'd kissed her, long before she'd recognized how adamant he was on the subject of permanent commitments, she'd known about that walled-off corner.

The knowledge had helped her keep her own balance because she in turn had never quite shut off the watchful guardian in her own brain. And perhaps that had been what saved her from the ultimate error of falling in love with him.

She'd unthinkingly assumed that the protective instinct of long ago would kick back into operation the moment she needed it. Instead, she'd lost her balance altogether. She'd been so out of control that she wasn't even certain where his actions had stopped and her own began.

And she was humiliated that he'd been the one who walked away before she'd had a chance to regain her senses and call a halt. As she would have done, given another minute or two.

She was certain of it.

To her chagrin, however, Deke had been the one to break free from that searing embrace. But why had he walked away? Had he felt triumphant because he'd made his point so effectively? Satisfied because he had nothing left to prove? Scared silly that she might misinterpret his motives?

Danielle wasn't so sure she wanted to know the answer.

At first, Danielle wasn't sure if the pounding she heard was real or imaginary. Was it caused by the questions still circling in her head, questions that had made her sleep choppy and unrefreshing? Or had a particularly athletic squirrel leaped onto the Merry Widow's roof?

But as she shook away her remaining sleepiness, she heard voices above her head, and everything came clear. The roofers, she thought. Odd that Deke hadn't mentioned last night that they'd be starting....

Or perhaps it wasn't odd at all, she reminded herself. She had completely forgotten to tell him about his message from Norah, hadn't she?

She pushed herself out of bed and went downstairs to fix the businessman's breakfast. Coffee and toast, he'd requested. Well, that was easy enough; she just hoped the roofers hadn't awakened him. She was already feeling guilty because he was paying for a complete breakfast and getting only toast and coffee.

But that's his own choice, isn't it? she could almost hear Pam asking. *Guests know when they make reservations that they're paying for breakfast. It's up to them whether they eat it.*

Pam was right, of course. "Maybe I should take a few lessons in cold-bloodedness from her," Danielle muttered. Not that Pam was harsh or unfair, and no one would ever call her penny-pinching. She was just self-confident and assertive.

But the roof was a completely different matter. Danielle

couldn't in all conscience charge a guest full price for an interrupted night's sleep.

The businessman assured her, however, when he came downstairs in a neat pin-striped suit, that he'd been up long before the noise started. Danielle breathed a sigh of relief, accepted his check, saw him off to meet with his client, then sat down with her own coffee.

Even in the kitchen, she could hear the banging two full floors above her head, and every now and then a bundle of shingles and other debris whooshed down the chute the roofers had rigged and crashed onto the concrete behind the house. Wondering if she should block off the area so the guests she was expecting that afternoon didn't park too closely, she took her coffee out to decide what she'd need. But if the sprawling heap of broken shingles wasn't warning enough to any person with ordinary sense, the cloud of dust that greeted her seemed to be. Danielle's eyes stung and she almost choked on the taste of it.

The dust cleared a bit, and she saw the contractor standing well back from the house with binoculars trained on the roof. Curious, she followed his gaze up to where the steep-sloping shingles met the wall of the square tower on the back corner of the house. As Danielle watched, a workman put his head over the edge. "Hey, boss! It's worse up here than you thought!"

Her heart sank. It had been difficult enough to accept the fact that through no choice of her own she owed Deke a sizable debt and had no way of repaying it till the Merry Widow was sold. But if that debt grew...and if there wasn't a sale soon...

She watched as the contractor scrambled up the ladder and strolled across the roof as easily as if he was walking down a hall. She watched as he moved around the tower, pointing now and then, giving instructions she couldn't hear from so far below.

Then he headed toward the ladder once more, and Danielle lost her nerve and went back inside. If there was bad news, she thought, let him break it to Deke himself instead of using her as the messenger. She knew she was being chickenhearted but also practical; what did she know about roofs anyway? And she certainly couldn't approve further work without Deke's okay.

Another load of debris bumped down the chute, shingles grinding and old nails squealing against the metal. The sound grated against Danielle's eardrums, and she picked up her keys and headed for the front door. She didn't know where she was going, but she couldn't stand much more of this.

Though it was still early, the square was full of people. Most of the shops hadn't yet opened, but the government offices in the courthouse must be doing a booming business. The historical society building was dark; though the museum wasn't scheduled to open till afternoon, Danielle took a good look, half-expecting to once again see Martha stranded. Hanging from a light fixture she was trying to clean, perhaps.

In front of the building that housed Deke's apartment, the owner of the antique store occupying the street level was setting a spinning wheel out on the sidewalk. She paused to eye Danielle and then said, "Deke hasn't gone out yet this morning. At least, his car's still behind the building."

Danielle wanted to say, *And what makes you think I might be interested*? Then she remembered the roofer and wondered if she owed Deke a warning.

"Thank you," she murmured, and walked around the corner to the side of the building and the entrance to Deke's private quarters.

A section of the old brick wall had been carved away and replaced with glass from sidewalk to roofline. She rang the bell beside the glass door and entertained herself while she waited by studying the scene inside. The foyer was tiny, just large enough for a black cast-iron spiral staircase and an infinitesimal elevator, which Danielle had thought an incredible affectation until Deke pointed out that it—along with the glass wall—had been installed by the elderly couple who'd lived there before him. The foyer floor was shiny black tiles laid in a subtle diamond pattern, the walls plain white and completely without decoration. The effect should have been stark and sterile and cold, but instead, the constant play of light against glass, metal and tile created a piece of modern art that changed from minute to minute. Sunlight made rainbows dance through the room, while on rainy days the clouds seemed to come inside. And the light of a full moon filled the space with pooled gold....

Danielle had first seen the apartment on a moonlit night, just a couple of weeks after she'd started seeing Deke more than casually. He'd come to the Willows for a late dinner, after most of the crowd had left, and offered her coffee afterward. She'd walked through a foyer kissed with warm gold light and she'd been kissed, in fact, in the elevator. When the door opened and she remembered where she was, she'd looked around the enormous space with something close to disappointment. She'd hoped the apartment would tell her more about Deke; one could learn a great deal by studying the things with which a person chose to surround himself.

Instead, the great room—a combination of living and dining rooms and media center, with a kitchen area off in a corner separated from the rest only by a huge stone fireplace—resembled an ad from some glossy magazine. The glamorous decor wasn't at all the sort of thing she'd expected Deke to care about. It wasn't till later she'd learned that he'd bought the place furnished, complete with the art on the walls, when the elderly owners had moved into the residential care facility on the outskirts of town. And by then she'd felt she knew Deke so well that she didn't need to search for clues.

Ah, what innocence! she thought, and rang the bell again.

This time, the answer coming from the speaker above the doorbell button was prompt. "Yes?" Deke's voice sounded a bit tinny over the intercom.

"It's Danielle. May I come up?" The ensuing silence was so long that Danielle grew annoyed. "Look, if you've got belly dancers up there, just tell me. You don't have to try to smuggle them out. I'll come back some other time."

Deke's laugh was almost drowned out by the buzz that released the lock. Danielle slipped inside and climbed the spiral stairs to the balcony forming the upper foyer. The view was even better from there; looking down at the shifting bars of light might be dizzying, but it was never dull. Still, she paused only an instant before crossing the balcony and turning the corner into the great room that occupied the front half of the apartment.

The room still reflected the taste of Elmwood's most popular decorator, though here and there Danielle could see cracks in the perfection. She was certain, for instance, that the decorator would never have approved Deke's use of the heavily carved library table to house his computer.

Though, Danielle thought, why *was* it in this room? The one area of the apartment where Deke had paid any attention at all to furniture and ambiance was the second bedroom, which he'd turned into his office.

Because, he'd said once when he'd been in a playful mood, the only people he ever invited to stay overnight didn't use the guest room anyway. She hadn't thought about that comment in months, and the sudden flash of memory sent warmth surging over her face.

Deke stood up from the computer table. Not only hadn't he gone out yet this morning, he didn't appear to be intending to, for he was barefoot, wearing jeans so faded they almost looked white and a Princeton sweatshirt that had also seen better days.

Even so, he looked great.

He came toward her, moving silently on the thick plush carpet. Although he was still ten feet away, she could feel against her hot skin the shift in air currents caused by his movement.

"Well, hello," he said softly. "Dare I hope, from that delightful little blush, that you came to finish what we started last night?"

"Of course not." The words were out before she considered that the denial itself was a confirmation of sorts—at least an admission that last night had not been an isolated incident, that someday it might be finished…. "Because last night didn't start anything at all."

The disavowal rang hollow in Danielle's own ears, like the feeble lie it was. For last night *had* changed a lot of things.

She'd always been highly aware of him—the way he moved, the lazy strength of his body, his sheer physical attractiveness. In the days when they'd dated, she'd gotten delicious shivers whenever he was near. After their split, the shivers had gone cold, but they were just as real. When Deke was in the room, she knew it—and she'd have known it blindfolded and in the dark, too.

But today it was different still. She felt as if each separate nerve in her body had been specially tuned to listen and respond to him and to nothing else—as if she had no reality, no function that didn't relate to him. She could feel his warmth, even from a distance of five feet. She could sense the tautness of his muscles. She knew that he was poised to move in any direction.

And she was horribly aware—now that it was too late to

leave—of the risk she had taken by coming to his apartment.

What frightened her was not the fact that he could overpower her with physical force—though he could, of course, if he chose. He'd done it before. On that far-too-memorable trip to the lake, she'd teased him about something silly, and he'd retaliated by easily picking her up and tossing her playfully off the float into the water.

But it wasn't the strength of Deke's body she was afraid of; it was the devastating sensations in her own. Merely looking at him not only brought back all the sensual memories of the night before, but it set her imagination afire with images of what could have—would have—come next....

He shrugged. "Have it your own way."

She hardly heard him, for her body was telling her how that shrug would have felt had she been touching him. The ripple of muscles under her hands, the rise and fall of his chest as he spoke, the rumbling vibration of his voice... Anticipation shivered down her spine.

As if there was anything to anticipate, she told herself. It was past time to get a grip on herself. She took a deep breath. "The roofers started this morning." She thought her voice sounded high and reedy.

"Good. The contractor said it'd just take a couple of days, so perhaps the work can be done before it rains again. Coffee?"

Danielle nodded, and he walked across to the kitchen and poured two cups from a thermal carafe. The farther away he was, she noted, the easier it was to breathe, so Danielle moved around behind an oversize couch and toward the windows overlooking the square.

Though she wasn't looking at him, she could almost count his steps as he crossed the room, for the hairs on the back of her neck acted as a sort of distance gauge. When she could stand the prickling sensation no longer, she turned to face him, and Deke handed her a coffee cup.

She managed to avoid the brush of his fingers. Not that it made a great deal of difference, since she not only knew already how firm and smooth and strong his hands were, but her brain had efficiently filed the knowledge where it could be easily cross-referenced from a dozen different directions—whether she wanted to be reminded or not.

She sat down on the very edge of a small chair. A moment later, seeing the flicker of amusement in Deke's eyes, she slid back into a more comfortable position, trying to look nonchalant.

"Make yourself at home," Deke murmured. He settled into a wing chair nearby.

"I don't think you should count on the roofers being done in a couple of days," Danielle said. "They seemed to think this morning that the damage was a whole lot worse than it looked before." She sipped her coffee. "I thought I should warn you that the contractor may be getting in touch."

"So that's why you came to visit?" He didn't wait for an answer. "Don't worry about it. The bid we got is a binding contract."

Danielle frowned. "So if there's hidden damage, he just has to fix it for free? That doesn't seem fair."

"Having trouble making up your mind? Contractors always build in some flexibility for unforeseen problems or they'd be out of business in about two weeks flat. If it's dramatically worse, he'll tell us—and we can amend the contract, make a new one or decide not to go ahead with the work after all."

"That's hardly an option. The roof's gone already on the back wing."

"Well, don't panic. I'm sure—"

"Who's panicking?" Danielle let a tinge of irony creep

into her voice. "And what reason do I have to be worried anyway? Just because there's daylight coming in through the ceiling of the back wing and dust an inch thick all over every piece of furniture in the house—oh, and the strawberry festival starting on Friday and every room spoken for, including the ones without roofs—"

"The crew will be done by then, I'm sure."

"Well, I hope they leave a little leeway for getting things tidied up again." She paused, then asked hesitantly, "Have there been any applicants for the housekeeping job?"

"A couple that Mrs. Baker didn't think were suitable."

"Oh, that's comforting. I'm so desperate I'd probably hire an orangutan if a willing one came along, so I'm glad to know she's protecting me from my own folly."

Deke grinned, and the sparkle in his eyes made Danielle's stomach do a sudden back flip. "I'll ask whether she can give you the rest of the week."

"That would certainly help." Her stomach was taking its own sweet time in settling down again. She let spurious concern drip from her voice. "As long as you're positive you can do without her, Deke. After all, the Merry Widow's needs pale beside yours."

"Just for that, I should leave her here and come over myself."

"Thanks anyway," Danielle said hastily. "But—"

"Don't you want to see me prove how efficient I can be in a bedroom?" Pure wickedness gleamed in Deke's eyes.

His voice, low and husky, promised a world of delights. But last night he had walked away.... *There isn't a serious cell in his body*, Danielle told herself. *And don't you forget it.*

She cleared her throat. "I've been meaning to ask whether you've heard of anyone interested in buying it."

"Changing the subject, Danielle?"

She tried to ignore him. "I've been so busy running the

place that I haven't even had time to listen to gossip lately.''

''Too bad. It's been extraordinarily interesting this week.''

She refused to take the bait. ''So if there's been any talk about possible buyers, I haven't heard it,'' she said crisply. ''I know it's really only been a few days, but I thought perhaps someone might have hinted at an interest. Maybe even gotten in touch with you.''

''I wonder if you actually expect the interested parties to form a line on the front porch, cash in hand.''

''I'm not that unrealistic. But it only takes one buyer.''

''And if that one is the apartment developer who gave us a bid last time?''

Danielle bit her lip. She felt just as strongly as she ever had about preserving the Merry Widow. But a year ago, the sales price hadn't mattered. If she'd ended up without a penny in her pocket, she wouldn't have cared. This time around, she didn't have the luxury of considering only her ideals. In debt, with a roof to pay for and no resources to fall back on, she couldn't lightly refuse any cash offer.

If the only potential buyer wanted to cut the Merry Widow into apartments or even tear it down for salvage…

The idea sent a shudder of revulsion through her. But she realized that if they had to agree on an answer to that question, this time it would be Deke who held the advantage.

He obviously saw the war going on within her. ''As a matter of fact, I haven't talked to the man in months. And I haven't gone looking for him because I doubt he's interested anymore. Since he started building that complex on the west edge of town…''

Relief percolated through Danielle.

''Don't get too complacent,'' Deke warned. ''I *have* contacted a couple of real-estate people, and they both told me that if we had a hundred buyers we couldn't do a thing. You were right about the Jablonskis. Since they officially haven't deserted the place, we can't even list it, much less agree to a sale.''

''The mortgage payment's due today,'' Danielle pointed out.

''Are you planning to sit beside the mailbox and wait for the check to arrive?''

''Of course not. But if they don't make a payment—''

''It still doesn't mean we can act any time soon. Not everybody who's late with a check is a deadbeat—and there are restrictions on what a creditor can do.''

''So we're stuck.''

''This is not news,'' Deke reminded her.

''I know.'' She sighed. ''You saw this coming, didn't you? That's why you thought I was being a Pollyanna about the whole thing.''

''Which time? When you insisted on holding the paper so Joe and Kate could buy the Merry Widow in the first place, or when they skipped town and you decided to take over?''

''All right, you don't have to rub it in.''

''Actually,'' Deke went on dispassionately, ''the second time around, you were more like Don Quixote than Pollyanna.'' He stood up. ''Another cup of coffee?''

''No, thanks.'' While he crossed the room to the kitchen, she stared out the window, and then called, ''What if we can find Joe and Kate?''

Deke paused with the coffeepot in midair. ''And do what? Twist their arms till they sign a quit-claim deed?''

''At least talk to them. Find out what their intentions are.''

''I've already authorized a sort of minor-league search.'' He came back toward the front of the apartment. ''But they're adults, and if adults want to disappear—separately or together—and break off contact with friends or relatives, they've got a right.''

"Just like that?" Danielle said doubtfully.

"There's no evidence that they didn't leave voluntarily. On the contrary, in fact—Joe made his intentions absolutely clear. If we tried to file a missing-persons report on them, the FBI would laugh us right out of the office.''

"I'll start asking at the Willows. Somebody has to have an idea of where they might have gone. Though I still wonder about Kate, you know.'' Danielle stared moodily across the room. "Just because Joe left town—"

"Doesn't mean she did,'' Deke finished. "You mean you're suspicious because of the bloodstains on the front-hall floor under the Oriental rug, and the recently disturbed dirt behind the carriage house?''

"*What*?''

"Both purely imaginary, I assure you. Just like the rest of the murder mystery you're concocting in your head.''

"Murder mysteries!'' Danielle snapped her fingers. "With guests participating and trying to solve the crime. I knew if you ever put your mind to this, Deke, you'd be a natural at the bed-and-breakfast trade.''

He looked, she thought with satisfaction, a little as if he'd been smacked over the head with a sledgehammer. Her good nature restored, she stood up, intending to carry her cup back to the kitchen and then say goodbye. But some imp in the back of her brain pushed her one step further. She paused beside his chair and playfully patted him on the head.

She'd forgotten, for that one vital moment, that just because she'd grown somewhat accustomed to the level of electricity in the room didn't mean that the voltage had gone down. The contact, simple as it was, brought back every ounce of the awareness that had paralyzed her earlier. The air currents between them seemed to pulse.

Deke reached up to capture her hand. Slowly, he rose till he loomed over her.

The only physical contact between them was the living bracelet formed by his fingers around her wrist. But the cloud of energy encircled her more tightly yet, sending electrical impulses racing madly along every nerve, stimulating and contradicting, arousing every cell....

Overwhelmed and frightened, with her heart skittering as wildly as if a pacemaker had gone awry, Danielle pulled away. Once more, distance helped a little; she retreated toward the foyer and the spiral stairs that would take her to the street, to fresh air, to sanity.

"Danielle," he said.

She paused. His voice was as inviting as a mirage, as dangerous as quicksand. She had to fight off the urge to turn back to him. "What?"

"Are you planning to take that coffee cup with you?"

She looked down; though her knuckles were white from her hold on the cup, she had forgotten it entirely.

He was coming closer. She held the cup out to him and took a quick step back.

Deke stopped. He looked down at the bit of pottery cradled in his hand and then at her. "When you make up your mind, Danielle," he said, "I'll be right here. Waiting."

She gathered the last of her poise and managed to smile and shrug. "What a relief it is to have that clear," she said sweetly. "You've been a bit contradictory, you know. After what happened last night—"

"Because I didn't take you up on the invitation to make love to you?"

"There was no invitation," she said sharply.

"The hell there wasn't. You weren't clearheaded enough to know what you were offering. That's why I left. When you come to me, Danielle, I want to be damned sure you know what you're doing and that you aren't smelling orange blossoms in the distance.''

As if she could still be so deluded, Danielle thought. ''You're almighty sure of yourself.''

''You know what you want. I'm just waiting for you to get honest enough to admit it.''

''And agree to your terms. Do you really think that's going to happen?''

''Of course, my dear.'' Deke's low, husky voice was like pumice against her skin—slightly abrasive, but exhilarating at the same time. ''I'm betting on it.''

CHAPTER EIGHT

THE Willows should have been a refuge. The lunch crowd was a light one, and there was plenty of help, so for a change Danielle wasn't pressed into changing table linens and refilling water glasses.

Or perhaps that was part of the problem—the fact that she had too much time on her hands to think about what had happened that morning in Deke's apartment. Because simply thinking about the crazy way she'd reacted to him was enough to send her spinning off in circles again.

I'll be right here. Waiting, he'd said. *When you make up your mind...*

As if there was anything to consider!

He'd made himself perfectly plain. She knew he still saw commitment as nothing more than a concept, one that didn't apply to him. She had no illusions left where he was concerned.

As for that remark about smelling orange blossoms...well, only an idiot would mention weddings and Deke Oliver in the same breath. Only an idiot, Danielle told herself, would even *want* to—and she wasn't that foolish.

But the truly crazy part was that she still couldn't quite dismiss his invitation from her mind.

You know what you want, he'd said. And every sinew of her body had tightened in the knowledge that he was right. She did want him.

But wanting was one thing; acting on that desire was another. Wanting was understandable. There was no denying the sheer magnetism of the man, and no question that

125

he'd been deliberately focusing every seductive talent he possessed on her. But acting on that desire...well, there were faster ways to self-destruct, but offhand, Danielle couldn't think of any surer ones.

Still, when she thought of him, her mouth went dry and her knees shook, and she could actually hear his quiet, husky voice echoing in her head. *I'm betting on it*, he'd said. *I'm just waiting...*

Pam looked up from the cash register drawer. "That was an Academy-Award-winning groan, Danny. In fact, you sound about as irritable as I feel. The Merry Widow again?"

Danielle seized at the excuse. "Oh, it's just that I'm here accomplishing nothing when there's so much still waiting to be done there. All I can do is make mental lists of all the chores that need to be done before the festival starts Thursday."

Pam rolled her eyes. "Please don't remind me of the festival. Just this morning, the wholesale grocer called to cheerfully tell me he can't supply me with all the petits fours I ordered for the historical society's tea tent—even though I told him almost six months ago that I'd need thirty dozen, and he assured me it would be no problem. Well, for him it may be no problem. For me—let's just say I'm not looking forward to mass-producing pastries in my cubbyhole of a kitchen."

"I'll bet Dad can think of another source."

"Ask Harry? Today? You must be joking."

Danielle was startled. "Why? What have I missed? He's back in the office right now, isn't he?"

"Yes, and why do you think I'm trying to count the drawer out here, where it seems I'm interrupted every time I get to fifty, instead of taking it in there?"

"Good question," Danielle admitted. "I hadn't realized—"

"Which just goes to show you how preoccupied you are that you didn't even notice Harry's mood. He's been walking around all morning as if he's not quite sure where he is, and when he settled into the office and started muttering to himself, I thought it was time to get out."

"His heart again." It wasn't a question.

Pam shook her head. "You know, I don't think it's physical. He looks fine except for the black cloud hanging over his head." She eyed Danielle. "So what's the problem at the Merry Widow that's keeping your mind too occupied to notice Harry?"

Danielle was still thinking about her father. "The place will be packed tight this weekend. In fact, I've had to turn down reservations." Which was another thing, she reminded herself. She hadn't been able to reach the woman who'd wanted two rooms for the entire weekend. "There'll be more guests than I've had to deal with before, and it scares me. That's all, really."

Pam's tone was more sympathetic than her shrug. "It just looks overwhelming. But doubling the number of guests doesn't really double the work, you know."

"It triples it instead?" Danielle asked, wide-eyed.

Pam grinned. "No, it only feels that way. Actually, Danny, I'd have thought the Merry Widow would be right down your alley. With all the experience you've had here of making people feel welcome and feeding them well—"

"I expect that's why I plunged into it so thoughtlessly," Danielle mused. "I mean, it should be just like having house guests, and what's so difficult about that? But it turns out to be a whole lot different when they're paying."

"You'd be considerably more cheerful about it if you felt settled. If you had your own furniture, for instance, instead of living with Kate's. If you had a sense of permanence, I'll bet you'd—"

"Heaven forbid." Danielle's voice sounded as hollow as

she felt. "It already feels a little too permanent for my taste. And the way things are beginning to look, it's going to be months yet before I can even think about going back to school—" She paused as the tiny bell above the door chimed, signaling a new customer. But the welcoming smile she'd assumed faded a bit when she saw who it was. "Hello, Kevin."

He looked a bit grim, she thought. If it hadn't been for the events of last night, she'd have suspected he was on his way to the dentist with a heck of a toothache.

"Will someone be joining you?" she added hopefully.

"You, I hope," he said.

Pam's head had come up at the sight of Kevin, and now her eyebrows arched.

"I knew better than to come by the Merry Widow." He sounded disgruntled. "Pam, you wouldn't mind watching things here for a while, would you? Just so Danielle and I can talk?"

Pam pursed her lips and looked thoughtful, and Danielle managed a tiny, discreet head shake. Pam said gently, "You know, Kevin, I didn't realize you were the new boss around here. Harry hasn't mentioned that I should start taking orders from you."

"I was only asking a favor," Kevin grumbled. "Though it's probably not a good idea. The last thing I need is for that arrogant so-and-so to see us together and draw the wrong conclusion again."

"Again?" Pam asked innocently. "We're talking about Deke, I assume? And what exactly were you doing the last time he drew the wrong conclusion?"

Kevin scowled. "Dammit, Pam, if you won't take over so Danielle can leave, how about you going away for a little bit?"

Danielle couldn't blame him for being annoyed; at the moment, she wouldn't mind throwing something at Pam herself. "Look, Kevin," she said briskly, "I really don't think there's anything we need to talk about, so why don't we simply agree that you apologized nicely and I accepted and we parted as friends?"

Kevin drew himself up straight. "Because I didn't come to apologize and I'm certainly not here to wish you happy. I think you've cracked up, Danielle. But there's obviously no talking to you about it, so it's just as well that your chaperon isn't going anywhere." He headed for the door but turned back to toss a parting shot. "Did Deke hire her to keep an eye on you when he couldn't be around, I wonder?"

He'd have slammed the door, Danielle was certain, if it had been possible.

"Wish you happy?" Pam sounded doubtful. "And what's this about you needing a chaperon?"

"That's not quite what he said. In any case, it's really another example of Kevin's gift for creative fiction." Danielle groped for a change of subject. "You know, Pam, if you're going to end up baking goodies for the tea tent yourself—"

"What I'd really like to do is borrow Harry's pastry chef, but he seems to have his hands full just now, too."

"You could come to the Merry Widow. The kitchen's pretty old, but there's plenty of space, and the oven seems to work fine."

"It's a shame Joe never got around to remodeling it."

Danielle considered. "Yes and no. If he had, I'd probably be up to my neck in party reservations. As it is, all I do is make sure the guests get a glimpse of the kitchen. They take one look, they're properly sympathetic—and they stop expecting a gourmet breakfast."

Pam laughed. "Trust you to find the good side. I just might take you up on the offer if you really don't mind having me in the way. As long as I'm baking, I could do a few things for your breakfasts, too.''

"A payoff isn't necessary, but I'm not nutty enough to turn you down.''

Pam's brows drew together. "The problem is... Would you mind awfully if I brought the kids? When Greg can't watch them, I mean. Maybe you can put them to work. They're not great at cleaning bathrooms and making beds, but with supervision—''

"I wouldn't expect them to pitch in.''

"Believe me, they're much more pleasant to have around when they've got a job to do, especially now that they're out of school. And since the sitter I thought I'd lined up for the summer pulled out because she got a better offer...''

Even if Danielle hadn't known what a disaster that news must have been, the tone of Pam's voice would have warned her. "Pam, what are you going to do?''

"I don't have an idea in the world. They're both at the awkward stage where nobody wants them—too old for day care, too young for jobs, and just old enough to get into plenty of trouble unless somebody's keeping an eye on them all the time.''

"Well, bring them along.''

"You really don't mind? At least they can empty wastebaskets and run the vacuum.''

"That's fine. But I meant here, too.''

"At the Willows? Harry would have to lock the kitchen or they'd eat him out of business. And that little problem would look mild compared to what some of my clients would have to say about my showing up with a couple of preteens in tow. I guess I'll make do with a patchwork of sitters again, but I was so hoping not to have to worry about it this summer.'' She flashed a smile at Danielle. "Maybe I should just trade you problems.''

There were times, Danielle thought, when she'd almost

be tempted by the offer. How much trouble could a couple of half-grown kids be anyway, compared to the mess she was in right now?

Of course, Danielle had to admit, it depended on the kids. Pam's two were a joy to have around; they fetched, carried, ran errands and even tried to help the roofers clean up the last of the mess after the work was finally done on Thursday, barely hours before the official start of the strawberry festival.

But the two groups of young people who checked into the Merry Widow with their parents late on Thursday afternoon were a little older and a lot less predictable. The three boys were just of an age to show off, impressing their new male acquaintances and pretending to ignore the female ones, while the two girls were at the awkward stage where they'd do nearly anything to attract the boys' attention. What had Kate been thinking of, to have booked them all at the same time?

Within minutes of his arrival, one of the boys slid down the banister headfirst, to the admiring coos of both of the girls. The banister creaked ominously, and his obviously long-suffering mother said weakly, ''Please, darling, what would Dad and I do if you broke the railing?''

''Pay for it,'' he said with a shrug. He slid off the newel post, landing face-to-face with Danielle. She didn't say a word, simply caught and held his gaze with an icy stare. His eyes dropped first, and she didn't think there'd be any more trouble from him where the staircase was concerned.

But there were plenty of other possibilities for an awkward adolescent determined to draw attention to himself, and Danielle couldn't possibly anticipate them all. She settled for retreating to the kitchen to stand guard over Pam's petits fours and tarts and tea cakes.

Pam's baking had filled the house with the richness of

chocolate and cinnamon and vanilla and nuts, scents that were bound to draw the attention and appetites of five kids. And if Pam came back from delivering her first load of goodies to the historical society's tent to pick up the second, only to discover her work had been decimated by a horde of two-legged locusts...

As she packed up the desserts, Pam had pushed aside a few misshapen tarts and lopsided petits fours. Danielle was arranging them in a box so they'd stay fresh when Deke came in the back door.

When she heard the door creak, she knew it was him by the prickling sensation that ran up and down her spine. She deliberately didn't look around, but kept setting tarts into the box. Stick to business, she told herself, just as she'd been doing for the past couple of days, and she'd be fine. "I was just about to call to see if you could come early," she began.

Deke's fingertips skimmed the sensitive skin at the back of her neck, and each hair seemed to stand up individually and demand attention. "Darling, what a surprise." His voice was no more than a rich murmur close to her ear, but Danielle could feel the vibrations clear to the end of her toes. "After the way you've been avoiding me lately, for you actually to request my company a full hour before you're due at the Willows—"

"I have not been avoiding you, Deke. I've been seeing you a half-dozen times a day."

Deke didn't answer, but the knowing little smile that tugged at the corners of his mouth made Danielle want to kick him. She hadn't even tried to avoid him; it would have been impossible to schedule her days to lessen the chance of running into him. With the strawberry festival due to start at sundown, the Merry Widow full to bursting and the list of dinner bookings at the Willows as long as her arm, the idea that she could plan her day around Deke's movements was too hilarious to contemplate.

She would have to admit, if she was pressed, that she was cautious about staying in the public areas of the house when he was around just in case he took a notion to try kissing her again. And she was downright grateful that Pam was popping in and out of the Merry Widow almost at random. But as for avoiding him...

Deke reached over her shoulder and snagged a lopsided cherry tart. ''If you see Pam before I do, tell her to let me know what she's charging for these,'' he said. ''So what brings about this invitation, Danielle?''

''Don't fool yourself—it isn't one. We have two pint-size temptresses in residence, along with three Tarzans, who by now have probably strung a rope from the highest tower window so they can pretend they're swinging through the jungle. Throw in one mother who's got the spine of a jar of jelly, another who's upstairs resting, two fathers who are nowhere to be found, and you've got the makings of a disaster.''

''And you want me to fix it?''

Danielle frowned. Had that note in his voice been apprehension or condescension? ''No, I just thought I should warn you before you walked in to find them using the parlor mantel as a balance beam.''

''Knocking heads together isn't allowed, I presume?''

''Child abuse.''

''Well, maybe I'm big enough to intimidate them.''

''Let's hope so. If they keep on the way they started, we'll be replacing the staircase before we even get the bill for the roof.''

''I don't hear any threatening thumps.'' He reached for a mug from the highest shelf of the cupboard. ''Is that fresh coffee?''

''Moderately.'' Danielle watched the way his polo shirt

strained as the muscles underneath tensed and relaxed, telling herself that she would have felt the same admiration for any other man with that physique.

And knew that she was lying.

With an effort, she dragged her attention off Deke's broad shoulders. "The lack of noise isn't necessarily reassuring, Deke. It isn't just toddlers who go quiet when they're up to something they shouldn't be."

He eyed her curiously. "And how do you know so much about it?"

"Didn't you ever baby-sit?" She didn't bother to wait for an answer. She pushed petits fours around to try to make room for one more in the box, then finally gave up.

Deke said with glee, "What a shame that there's one lonely cake left over. Well, we can't let it just sit there and dry up, can we?" He picked up the petit four and waved it toward the door. "Go on to work if you like. I'll keep an eye on things here."

Danielle eyed him warily. "Are you certain you can handle this?"

"So what's the problem? If they get too far out of hand, I'll just march them down the block to the day-care center and enroll them."

She couldn't possibly *not* go to work; the Willows was going to be as busy tonight as she'd ever seen it. And the kids who occupied the Merry Widow like an invading army were Deke's problem just as much as hers.

Deke put a fingertip under her chin and lifted till her gaze met his. "Stop looking at the place as if you'll never see it standing again," he ordered. He dropped a careless, featherlight kiss on her lips. "I'll handle it."

Danielle tried to stifle the shock waves that blasted through her, so he wouldn't see how rattled she was by that simple touch. But she saw his eyes narrow and knew that she hadn't been successful.

He leaned closer. "Not satisfied?" he whispered. "We'll have to correct that."

She was murmuring a protest when he kissed her, long and full, with no demands, no fierceness—so softly, in fact, that she found herself relaxing into his embrace, grateful for an uncomplicated kiss that asked nothing of her but enjoyment. As she gave back to him with the same simplicity, the passion that was lurking under that softness all along hit her like a ten-ton truck slamming into a brick wall. Her body ached under the force of it, and when he let her go, her head was spinning.

"That wasn't fair," she muttered, still too shaken to wonder if it was wise to say anything at all.

"No," he agreed. "But then, I never promised to play fair."

He never promised anything at all, Danielle reminded herself. In personal relationships—or even in financial ones, she reflected when she spotted Martha and a couple of other historical society members in the line waiting for tables at the Willows. Danielle would bet that, whatever Martha thought, he hadn't even come close to guaranteeing that the money she'd invested would continue to earn so well or even that it would still be there when Martha wanted it back.

Avoiding promises was something that Deke did very well indeed. And Danielle wasn't fool enough to forget it.

Eventually, as the early crowd finished their dinners and drifted out of the Willows and back toward the strawberry festival, she showed the historical society contingent to their table. "I'm starving," one of them said. "I've been watching over all those goodies in the tent for hours, and there wasn't a single thing there my doctor would let me eat."

"I'm sure we can take care of that problem, Hazel."

Danielle handed her a menu. "How are things going at the tent?"

"Everybody but Hazel's forgotten all about their diets," Martha said. "It looks like we'll nearly sell out before the festival closes down for the night."

"The good news," Hazel said, "is that we're making loads of money for the new exhibits we want to put up. The bad news is all of us are going to have to go home tonight and bake so we can open the tent again tomorrow."

Poor Pam, Danielle thought. She was sure she had plenty of goodies on hand.

"I'll make sure to stop by sometime," Danielle promised. "Enjoy your dinner. Sally will be right with you."

She returned to the maître d's stand to take another set of names—people without reservations who still hoped to get a table—and had just sent the group to the lounge to wait when Martha came up. She looked around as if to make sure no one could overhear and whispered, "I need to talk to you a minute, Danielle, about the museum."

She looked stressed, Danielle realized. And in fact, now that she thought about it, Martha hadn't been as enthusiastic about the tent's success as Danielle would have expected her to be. The woman had hardly met her eyes at all, and now she looked…sheepish, perhaps.

Danielle's heart sank. Had the trustees refused to go along with her decision to give museum money to Deke to invest? Had they perhaps censured Martha for going behind their backs? Her position with the museum was the most important thing in the woman's life; had they possibly even taken away her title and her keys?

Or worse, had Martha's investment strategy exploded already?

"It's the money," Martha went on. "You see, I…I misread the statement. You know, the one I was telling you and Pam about at her party. We didn't make nearly as much interest last month as I thought. Deke very kindly explained it to me.''

I'll just bet he was very kind, Danielle fumed.

''You see, I thought the last deposit we made into the fund was interest,'' Martha said. ''And I figured it all wrong, too. So instead of a hundred percent, we made…'' Her voice dropped even further. ''Two. Deke tells me that's still very good for just a month, and of course it helps that he's not charging us a fee at all, but I feel a bit… Well, here come more customers for you, and I have to get back to the table before they start wondering why I'm taking so long. You won't tell anybody about my silly mistake, I know.'' She hurried off before Danielle could answer.

So perhaps Deke hadn't been playing roulette with the museum's money, Danielle thought, or taking advantage of Martha's innocence to increase his own profits. No wonder he'd been a bit touchy about the subject of skimming money from the museum's funds—especially if he wasn't getting paid at all.

In that case, she owed him an apology. Another one.

A busboy brought back a stack of menus and told her about a now free table, so Danielle checked a name off her list and went to the lounge to retrieve the customers. When she came back, yet another foursome was waiting in the entrance.

She'd started to greet them when the welcoming words froze on her tongue—for the four included Norah and her parents…and Deke.

Danielle had little enough common sense left where he was concerned, and now fury burned up the remaining fragments. ''And who's looking out for the Merry Widow? Or was I hearing voices from outer space? I thought you said *you'd* keep an eye on things.'' Her tone should have turned him to cinders.

Deke lifted one eyebrow. ''I said I'd handle it and I did.

Pam's baking up a storm, and since she had to be there for a while yet, she offered to keep an eye on the guests. Most of them are off at the festival anyway.''

Danielle was somewhat mollified by the fact that at least he hadn't simply walked out. But she wasn't quite ready to let him off the hook. "Pam has enough to do."

"And she's doing it very well, too," Deke agreed. "Every time I walked through the kitchen I was making another donation to the historical society because there was another new treat I just had to sample."

"You have all my sympathy," Danielle said coolly. "It's a good thing you had a snack, though, as it'll be a while before I can seat you. If you don't mind waiting in the lounge..."

Norah's mother sniffed disdainfully, but she led the way. Her voice floated back to Danielle, however—as she no doubt knew it would. "The Willows *used* to have a pleasant staff."

Danielle bit her tongue. The reproof was certainly catty, but there was an edge of truth to it. She'd never had any trouble being pleasant and tactful, or diplomatically refusing to be drawn into controversial topics, until this week— but in the past seven days, she'd violated her own rule more times than she cared to count.

Of course, she'd also been pushed further in the past week than ever before. And tonight, when Deke had walked in with Norah just a few short hours after he'd kissed Danielle...

It wasn't the Merry Widow she'd been fussing about, she realized. It was the harsh reality that Deke had kissed Danielle as if there had never been another woman in the world and then turned up with Norah on his arm.

As if there had never been another woman in the world. The words struck hard and deep, for that had been her interpretation, not Deke's. She had once more allowed romance to color reality. She had let herself believe for that tiny span of time not only that she mattered to him, but that she was the only one who mattered.

And this time, she had drifted into that dream knowing full well how he felt about commitment, about permanence...about her. The knowledge that should have prevented such foolishness had not done so. It had not protected her as it had throughout the past year.

Or...had it ever protected her at all? Had she really escaped unscathed as she had told herself during the long months since their breakup, or had she simply refused to face the truth—that she had fallen in love with a man to whom she meant so little?

She hadn't even admitted to herself what an enormous dam of denial she had built inside her heart until seeing him with Norah tonight had allowed a crack to form in the concrete, a crack that let seep forth the truth that she loved him and that she had loved him for a very long time.

That was why she hadn't dated much in the year since their breakup—not because she was afraid to trust her judgment when it came to other men, as she had once told Pam, but simply because there was no other man who could compare to Deke. No other man whom she could love.

Not that admitting the truth was going to get her anywhere, Danielle thought bleakly. If he got so much as a hint of how she felt, Deke would be gone like a puff of smoke in a hurricane, and then she wouldn't even have the stolen, almost illicit pleasure of his kisses. She couldn't even bask in the knowledge that despite the limited terms he offered, he did want her.

And she certainly couldn't take a chance on anyone else guessing how she felt, sympathizing, perhaps even commenting. She would have to be very, very careful.

When the foursome's table was available, Danielle asked her father to seat them. Harry looked at her sharply but did as she asked. When he came back to the maître d's stand, however, he said, "Things have settled down a bit. I think that was the last of them." He pointed toward the office, a silent command.

Danielle shook her head. "I don't need a rest, really."

"Yes, you do. But that wasn't precisely what I meant. I need to talk to you, and between the festival and the Merry Widow, heaven knows when we'll have another chance."

Danielle groaned inside. The last thing she needed tonight was one of those concerned-father chats. What imp had prompted Harry to pick up on her mood tonight and insist on discussing it right now and right here? But she obeyed, choosing the chair facing the office door, which Harry had left open so she could see whenever a customer needed attention.

He sat down across from her, propped his elbows on the arms of his chair, tented his fingers and rested his chin on them, then simply looked at her.

Am I flashing announcements in neon? Danielle wanted to ask.

"How would you like to go back to school this summer?" he asked finally.

"You don't think you need me anymore?" Danielle forced a smile. "Since I've never officially been on the payroll, you can't exactly fire me, you know."

"Oh, no. I'll leave that for the new owner to do."

The words took a moment to sink into Danielle's preoccupied brain. "The new... You've sold the Willows?"

Harry nodded. "To a man who already owns a string of fine restaurants all around the state. In fact, you met him this week. He stayed at the Merry Widow when he came in to look over the Willows."

Danielle frowned. "You mean the businessman who only wanted toast and coffee is a restaurateur? Oh, that's funny."

"He'll put in a manager, and of course some things will change. But he's committed to keeping up the quality our customers have come to expect. And he's agreed to keep everybody on the staff at least through the transition period. Everybody but you and me, that is." He smiled wryly. "And I can see his point. It'll be hard enough for a manager to come in from outside without the old bosses still hanging around."

Danielle nodded, but she wasn't really listening. No wonder Harry had been restless and preoccupied. No wonder she'd found him poring over papers late at night. Dealing with a decision of that scope, entirely alone...

"Daddy, why didn't you tell me you were thinking about it?"

"I didn't want to get your hopes up till I had something firm to tell you."

"My hopes?"

"Of being able to leave here, go back to school. Live your own life again."

He heard what I told Pam the other day, Danielle thought, *about being frustrated over how long it's all taking. And he's been feeling guilty about it—as if it was his fault!* No wonder Harry had been in a black mood....

Wait a minute, she told herself. He'd been gloomy even before she and Pam had their chat, hadn't he?

She asked quietly, "Is that why you did it? Because you thought I felt trapped?"

Harry shook his head. "Not really. It's time to let go. I can't keep up the pace anymore, even with you to help. But I have to admit when I walk out that door for the last time, I might as well tear out a piece of my heart. It'll be like saying goodbye to your mother all over again." He rubbed his forehead and forced a smile. "No, I didn't do it because of you, Danielle. But you'll get a good piece of the sale price."

"No, Daddy."

The thin smile grew into a natural grin. "I insist. I'd rather give you a chunk than pay tuition—and obviously you'll need help after the way you've been giving away money right and left for the past year."

"Giving away money?" Danielle said carefully.

"Did you think I didn't know about the historical society? I've just never understood why."

The telephone rang, and Danielle gratefully rested a hand on the receiver. But before she picked it up, she answered her father. "Because if I hadn't given Miss Fischer the wrong idea, she'd have left the Merry Widow to them instead."

Harry rolled his eyes. "Danielle, you're a first-class idealist. Always have been, just like your mother. Now the way the real world operates—"

She smiled at him and picked up the phone, but before her first word was out, Pam's panicky voice twisted Danielle's stomach into a knot. "Danny, there's a woman here who says she has a reservation, but there's nothing in the book."

Danielle closed her eyes, trying to visualize the calendar. She hadn't added anything to Kate's schedule, but had she misread it? Surely Kate couldn't have overbooked—though if she'd been as preoccupied as Danielle suspected in the last weeks she'd run the Merry Widow, anything could have happened. Still, she hadn't noticed anything amiss when she'd planned the room assignments....

"And it's for two rooms," Pam went on.

The knot in Danielle's stomach tightened. *Surely it can't be the woman who called Sunday, the one I couldn't reach to tell her that there were no rooms left.*

"Please come quickly," Pam said flatly, "because I don't have a shadow of an idea how to deal with this Mrs. DeCarlo."

CHAPTER NINE

DANIELLE made it to the Merry Widow in record time, and before she was halfway down the hall to the most formal parlor, she could hear Mrs. DeCarlo—she recognized the clipped accent from the message the woman had left. "All I want," the woman was saying, "is to be shown to my room."

Danielle paused in the doorway, taking in the scene. Good for Pam, she thought; she'd brought the unexpected guest to the nicest area of the house, made sure she took the most comfortable chair and provided her with both a glass of wine and a selection of the best-looking petits fours a tea tent would ever boast.

The fact that Mrs. DeCarlo seemed to have ignored the wine and cakes and been unimpressed by the surroundings was beside the point.

Pam looked up, and relief swept across her face. "Here's the manager now."

Danielle thought Pam probably used the same soothing tone to a child who was about to get his shots. It had no effect on Mrs. DeCarlo, who twisted around in her chair and fixed a piercing gaze on Danielle. "It's about time that someone with the authority to solve this problem appeared. This young woman knows nothing." Her glance dismissed Pam as a nonentity.

"And she shouldn't be expected to," Danielle said. "Mrs. Lanning was simply helping me out."

"That's no way to run a business, leaving someone in charge who is obviously unqualified. I made reservations," Mrs. DeCarlo said ominously. "But she can't find them."

"You called for reservations," Danielle corrected. "And when I called back to tell you that the Merry Widow was already fully booked for this entire weekend, there was no answer."

"I can hardly be expected to sit beside the telephone and wait for an innkeeper to phone."

Danielle said levelly, "Then you shouldn't be surprised when the innkeeper doesn't have a room to spare."

"In a town like this? There can't be many people wanting to stay here."

"Unfortunately, you happened to choose the same week as our most popular tourist attraction. All of my guest rooms are already taken."

Mrs. DeCarlo's gaze shifted a bit to the side. "I told you not to accept that rental car."

Danielle blinked in surprise at the non sequitur. She followed Mrs. DeCarlo's look and for the first time realized that there was another woman in the room—a small, pale mouse whose entire attitude shrieked *companion*.

"If we hadn't had trouble with the car, we'd have been here hours ago," Mrs. DeCarlo went on, "and there wouldn't have been a problem. This is entirely your fault, Laura."

Danielle saw the mouse cringe and almost automatically she stepped in to defend her. "Getting here earlier today wouldn't have gotten you a room, Mrs. DeCarlo. All of the other guests had confirmed reservations weeks ago, and I'm not about to inconvenience them on your behalf. I don't know where you're going to find a place to stay, but..."

The mouse looked as if she was about to give way to panic, and Danielle paused instead of finishing, *but that's not my problem*. She couldn't ignore the poor woman's pain. Surely there had to be an alternative.

She glanced at Pam and said softly, "I don't suppose the Highway Motel..."

Pam looked horrified. "No."

Danielle couldn't blame her; she knew herself that she was grasping at straws. "The newer ones are both full," she said. "One of the managers called me yesterday to ask if the Merry Widow still had rooms. And the other was in the Willows for lunch today and said he'd just sold out this morning."

Which left only a small motel on the old highway outside the city limits—and both the building and the surroundings had seen much brighter days. Pam was right; it was out of the question.

"There might be space in the next town—"

"Probably not," Pam said. "It's the biggest strawberry festival we've ever had. It'll have to be the attic."

Danielle blinked. "I—"

"It's absolutely the only thing left," Pam murmured. "Sorry I didn't think of it before, Danny. They'll have to share, but it's a king-size bed, isn't it?"

"It's a pair of twins, actually, shoved together. But—"

"Even better. I'll run up and change the sheets right now."

A flood of gratitude warmed Danielle's heart, but Pam had vanished before she could say a word. How, she wondered, had she ever come to deserve a friend as loyal as Pam?

Mrs. DeCarlo said coldly, "Did she say the *attic*?"

On second thought, no wonder Pam had taken off so suspiciously fast. She wasn't simply efficient; she'd seen this one coming. "It's been converted into a very nice little suite," Danielle began. "The owners' own quarters, as a matter of fact."

"Young woman, if you think I'm sleeping in an attic…"

Danielle faced her squarely. "It's the only option I have to offer. If you choose not to accept it, feel free to go elsewhere."

A long silence filled the room, with only the mechanical ticking of the mantel clock to show how long the face-off continued.

Mrs. DeCarlo gave in first. Not that she admitted it, of course; Danielle hadn't expected her to. But there was a slight droop of her shoulders, a tiny shift in her chilly stare.

Danielle acted quickly. "I'm sure you'll be quite comfortable there. Is your luggage still in the car or have you brought it in?"

Leaning on both the railing and her companion, Mrs. De Carlo groaned all the way up the two long flights of stairs. She was giving an Oscar-winning performance, Danielle thought, and hoped it didn't wake the guests who had already settled in for the night.

At the top of the attic stairs, the mouse showed a spark of spirit. "Look how big it is, Georgina," she said. "This will be just lovely."

Mrs. DeCarlo sniffed, but she didn't squash the mouse as Danielle thought she might. "I assume," she told Danielle, "that tomorrow you'll make other arrangements."

Danielle smiled. "If two parties of guests leave unexpectedly early," she agreed sweetly, "you may certainly have their rooms." She ran a quick glance over the attic suite. Pam had not only changed the sheets, she'd pulled the sections of the bed off to the sides and moved a tiny table in between.

Danielle wished her guests a good night and retreated, catching up with Pam on the main stairs just in time to relieve her of an armload of used sheets and towels. She took the bundle straight to the laundry room, knowing that she'd need every clean sheet in the house tomorrow.

As soon as the washer started to chug, she went in search of Pam and found her in the front parlor lying on the fainting couch.

"I hope that fixed stare is only exhaustion," Danielle said as she tossed herself into a chair.

"What do you mean, *only* exhaustion? Next year, I swear, the moment anybody starts talking about the strawberry festival, I'm leaving town."

"No, you won't."

Pam sighed. "You're right. But I'm not volunteering for anything ever again."

"Does that mean even if you had a guest room, you wouldn't have offered to take Mrs. DeCarlo in for the night?"

Pam shuddered. "Take that barracuda home with me? She's worse than my mother-in-law." She sat up enough to reach for the glass of wine Mrs. DeCarlo had left untouched, then raised the glass in a salute. "White zinfandel, left to breathe a little too long and more than slightly warm against the palate. Nevertheless, it's just what the doctor ordered."

Danielle picked up a petit four. "I don't think I've eaten since lunch. The restaurant was crazy tonight."

"You know," Pam said thoughtfully, "now that you've brought it up, I can't get Harry out of my mind. Of course, there's nothing much to do but think when you're running cakes through an assembly line. But from the way he's been acting, if I didn't know firsthand how well the Willows has been doing financially, I'd say he's getting ready to close the place."

Danielle was startled. For a while, she'd actually forgotten about Harry's announcement—but of course Pam didn't know. "Close, no. Sell, on the other hand—"

"Is he really planning to?" Pam actually sat up at the news.

"He already has. He just told me tonight, and I don't know when he's going to announce it, so keep it under your hat, okay?"

"Well, isn't that just dandy? Not asking me to keep quiet, I mean, but the sale."

Danielle frowned. Then she realized that the sale would have its impact on Pam, too; the Willows was one of the larger clients of her independent accounting service. "I'm sorry, Pam. He did say the new owners will keep everybody on." The words rang hollow, however. The regular staff was one thing, but contracted help was different. And no doubt a businessman who owned a string of restaurants already had all the accountants he'd need.

Pam didn't answer.

One of the family groups who'd arrived that afternoon came through the front door. Danielle could hear a high, excited, childish voice, and a moment later one of the girls dashed into the parlor and pulled up short. "Isn't Deke here?" Her voice dripped disappointment.

"Sorry," Danielle told her. "You're stuck with me."

"You aren't bad," the girl said graciously. "But *Deke*…"

The hero worship in her voice amused Danielle. So that was how he'd handled the feminine portion of the show-off kids, was it? By allowing them to develop a crush on him? What had he done with the boys, she wondered. Taught them karate?

Pam lifted a hand just high enough to see her wristwatch, then let it fall. "He'd better show up soon," she said. "He promised to bring me a filet with all the trimmings."

Danielle wasn't surprised. "So he did bribe you to stay."

"Not really. I offered, and he said in that case, he'd make sure I got something besides petits fours to eat. And I told him to make it the best on the menu."

"No doubt he considered it a small price for being able to go have dinner with Norah."

Pam turned her head. "Danny, that comment makes you sound remarkably like a jealous cat."

Danielle bit her tongue, hard.

The girl said, "I'll just wait down here till he comes, if it's all right with you, Miss Evans."

From the hallway, her father expressed a differing opinion, and eventually the girl trailed off toward the stairs with her lower lip stuck out.

Almost before she was out of sight, Pam was clutching her sides in an effort not to laugh. Danielle was just grateful to the girl for distracting attention from her slip. She should never have mentioned Norah at all. The last thing she needed was Pam asking tough questions—even if they were loving ones.

A cheerful cry rang out from the first landing. "Deke!"

"The hero returns," Pam murmured. "I hope he's not going to let my filet get ice-cold while he collects a little adulation."

"It's *exactly* what he needs more of," Danielle agreed.

A couple of minutes later, Deke came into the parlor, carefully carrying the largest take-out box the Willows stocked. "Sorry it took so long, Pam," he said.

Was Norah especially demanding? Danielle wanted to ask. *And just what do you whisper while you're kissing her?*

She tried to force the questions away. Pam was right. She *was* acting like a jealous cat—and doing so would only make everything hurt worse. If others saw it...if *Deke* saw it...

"You missed all the fun," Pam told Deke. She opened the take-out box and started to nibble at the spicy fried potatoes arranged in a neat wreath around her steak. "The houseguest from hell checked in half an hour ago."

"I thought the place was packed full already."

"We put her in the attic," Pam said. "I think that in the dead of night, Danielle should go out to the carriage house and see if she can find a chain for the door." She frowned.

"Except, of course, that would mean keeping her around even longer."

"She wanted to book for the whole weekend," Danielle offered. "When she called originally, I mean."

"*Definitely* you should add a chain. You can take it off on Monday morning. How was Norah's party, Deke?"

"Like most of them. A bit awkward."

I'll bet, Danielle thought. *What with meeting the parents and all, it must have been mighty awkward—especially for somebody like Deke.*

And that, she told herself, showed precisely how difficult it was going to be not to let jealousy get the best of her.

"Well, that's to be expected, I suppose." Pam picked up the take-out box. "In the meantime, I have one more batch of cakes to bake and ice. Which means I'll be around for hours yet—and since there's no place for either of you to spend the night comfortably, you might as well go get some sleep." Her voice was bland. "Separately or together. It's immaterial to me." She whistled softly as she walked down the hall toward the kitchen.

"Funny," Danielle said. "Pam's quite the comedienne." She jumped up. "Most of the guests are back now and settled in, so…"

She didn't actually see him move, but suddenly Deke was between her and the parlor door. "Is it really so funny?" he asked softly. "The idea that you and I might find some joy together?"

Inside her mind there seemed to be a tangled mass of threads, each one a separate emotion. Love, desire, anger, confusion, resentment, all twisted together into an insoluble knot. But the one image that overwhelmed all the others was of him tonight, coming into the Willows with Norah—and her parents….

She kept her voice steady. "Yes, it's funny."

He looked down at her for a long time and then stepped

aside so he was no longer blocking the door. "Good night, Danielle."

It felt, she thought, a whole lot more like goodbye.

He followed her down the hall to the side entrance, where Danielle turned to the kitchen door, and Deke went out.

Pam turned the mixer off just as Danielle came in. "Are you still here?" Her gaze flicked on past Danielle as if she expected to see Deke standing behind her.

"Right, Pam." Danielle didn't even try to stifle the irony in her voice. "Of course I'm going to spend the night with him. Just because the man went out to dinner with another woman is no reason to carry a grudge—"

"It's not like it was a date, Danielle."

"What, because her parents were there? Let me tell you, where Deke's concerned that's way more meaningful than the average date."

Unruffled, Pam tipped her mixing bowl over a cake pan and poured the batter out in a steady stream. "It was a farewell party."

He's leaving. The thought was like a knife to Danielle's chest. Just days ago, she'd asked Deke why he'd come to Elmwood and why he'd stayed. Nevertheless, the idea that he might actually leave ripped at her.

Of course, things had changed a little since then, she admitted. Or, perhaps it was more accurate to say that her knowledge of herself had grown.

"Norah's husband wants to reconcile," Pam went on, "so she's on her way back to California tomorrow."

It wasn't Deke who was going after all? Danielle managed to keep the relief out of her voice but only by reminding herself how often such stories turned out to be mere speculation. "Says who? Mrs. Hansen and the rest of the Elmwood gossip chain?"

"Among others. Including Norah's mother."

The pain in Danielle's chest had eased enough for her to draw a deep breath. Still...wasn't there something missing? Something that didn't fit? "She's going back to her husband," she said. "So she had dinner her last night here with Deke. Oh, that makes perfect sense. Except—why Deke?"

"I'm not sure," Pam said placidly. "It was Norah's father who called and asked him to come. My guess is that the man felt outnumbered. Wouldn't you, with both Norah and her mother to deal with?"

That still didn't quite answer the question, Danielle decided. *Why Deke?* But it did lead her thoughts in a new direction. If he'd been romancing them both, would Deke have had the nerve to bring Norah to the Willows tonight— when he knew perfectly well Danielle would be there?

Maybe, she supposed. It was a given that he didn't feel any commitment to her. So why should he feel any restrictions where other women were concerned? Perhaps he'd even done it on purpose, to make absolutely certain that Danielle couldn't fool herself into believing that anything he offered would turn into more than a casual fling.

She felt as if she'd taken an unexpected leap from a bridge and was now bouncing up and down on a bungee cord.

"Well, wherever you're going," Pam said, "run along, will you? I'll be here anyway."

"I shouldn't leave you with the responsibility." But Danielle's protest was halfhearted.

"There's no place for you to sleep. And you're going to need your rest because—let me make this very clear—I did *not* volunteer for breakfast duty."

Danielle grinned. "All right. I'm gone."

She was almost out the door when Pam added, with a twinkle in her eye, "One last question, Danny. If the maniac breaks loose from the attic and I need you—where shall I call?''

Danielle made a face at her and pulled the door shut.

The main events of the strawberry festival were being held at Elmwood's largest park, blocks away from the downtown area. But there was more traffic than she'd expected on the square, and she was held up when the street was blocked by a couple of drivers apparently uncertain of where they were going. As she waited for them to make up their minds, Danielle tapped her fingers on the steering wheel and looked up at the square.

The lights were on inside the glass foyer of Deke's apartment, turning the narrow two-story space into a beacon worthy of a lighthouse. With each heartbeat, the beacon seemed to pulsate—but instead of a lighthouse warning her away, the brilliance seemed to act as a magnet, drawing her closer.

There was a glow from the bay window in the living room, as well. Obviously, Deke was still awake, and up.

Traffic cleared, but Danielle didn't take her foot off the brake.

She'd had good intentions of apologizing for misjudging him where Martha and the museum were concerned. No wonder she'd forgotten, though, with the twin blows of seeing him with Norah and realizing how she felt about him, topped off by Harry's news and the scene with her demanding guest. And, as if none of that had been enough, there was the casual way Deke had asked her to go to bed with him. It was hardly surprising Martha had been pushed to the back of her mind.

Still, she *did* need to apologize. And with all the frenzy of the festival, with the Merry Widow packed full, it wouldn't be easy to find time for a private word. Besides, she admitted, after that oddly final parting tonight, he might not give her much of a chance.

She didn't realize a car had come up behind her until the driver tapped his horn impatiently. Almost without thinking, she turned onto the square and found a parking spot across from Deke's building.

The lights in the bay window died as she passed underneath, and she almost lost her nerve. But she pressed the doorbell anyway and waited for the intercom.

When he answered, he sounded tired, she thought. "Deke? Can I have a minute?"

The only reply was the buzzer sounding, releasing the lock.

He was waiting at the top of the spiral stairs, leaning against the railing, watching her. Danielle found herself suddenly out of breath as if she'd been climbing a sheer cliff instead.

He didn't move until she reached the landing, then he stepped back and gestured toward the living room. "Come in."

"I won't stay," she said.

"What a pity." His voice was dry.

Danielle felt warmth rising in her face. She'd meant it only in the polite sense, and Deke must know that perfectly well.

"I meant you must be tired, so I won't keep you." That pleasantry wasn't going to turn out any better, she realized, and stopped.

To her relief, Deke didn't bother to respond.

The living room was dark except for the spillover of the streetlights on the square, which filtered through the thin curtains and played tag against the plain white walls. The dimness might make it easier to say what she needed to, she hoped, and took a few more steps into the room before she turned to face him.

"I'm sorry to disturb you," she began.

"It's nothing. I was just finishing up some things for Norah to take with her tomorrow."

Pam had been right, then. Well, wasn't she usually? Danielle told herself it was foolish to feel so pleased. Norah's leaving didn't mean that Danielle's wishes were closer to coming true.

"I talked to Martha tonight," she said tentatively. "She told me about misreading the statement—the one on the museum's investments." She forced a smile. "Martha's a sweetheart, but she's no threat to the wizards of Wall Street, that's sure."

Deke didn't answer.

Suddenly, Danielle wished she'd stayed in the light, where she'd have had a better chance of reading the expression in his eyes.

"I should have known, though, that you wouldn't have done what it seemed you had. I'm sorry, Deke."

He moved slightly. "Perhaps I should ask for the list of your suspicions before I decide whether to accept this apology. Was it just overrisky investing you suspected me of, or active fraud?"

He's not going to make this easy, she realized. But then, why should he? "A little of both, I think," she said quietly. "Until I had a chance to consider, and then I knew there must be an explanation. It was a relief tonight when Martha told me what had happened, but not a surprise."

"I didn't know she was acting without the trustees' approval."

"I sort of expected that."

He stood for a moment without speaking, then nodded.

It was amazing, Danielle found, how much that tiny gesture could mean—and what a comfort it was to know that she'd done her part to clear the slate, and he'd accepted the effort.

It was time to leave. But her feet seemed glued to the carpet.

Because I don't want to go.

She told herself not to be ridiculous. Nothing had changed, really. Yes, she knew now how she felt about him—knew that she had loved him for a very long time. But loving him was hopeless, and making love with him would be the ultimate foolishness.

Wouldn't it?

It would devastate her to give herself so completely to him, knowing that sooner or later she would have to stand silent and watch him turn away. It would break her heart to have to see him after it was over—perhaps even to watch him with other women....

She managed two shaky steps toward the foyer. "Well, that's all I came for."

He didn't move aside to let her pass. "Is it, Danielle?"

His voice had a rough edge that she'd never heard before, and it scraped against her skin like sandpaper, setting every nerve quivering.

He lifted one hand as if to cup her cheek, but instead of touching her, his fingertips stopped a bare inch away. Despite the distance, she could feel his touch.

I won't have to watch him turn away, she realized. *Because I'm the one who'll be leaving.* She wouldn't be there to see the other women in his life.

She'd be staying in Elmwood until the Willows changed hands, of course—but that would be a matter of a few weeks and maybe far less. It might take a little longer to make long-term plans for the Merry Widow. They could hire a manager, perhaps, until the Jablonski problem could be solved. And then she'd be gone—back to Chicago in plenty of time to start the fall term.

So why shouldn't she take advantage of this hole in time to give herself some memories to treasure—and the knowledge that once, for a brief span, she had been near the center of his world?

He never makes promises. She knew that. Now, in a moment of quiet decision, she stopped fighting the facts. She felt no resignation, no resentment, no sense of loss. Deke was what he was, and she loved him in spite of it. Perhaps, just a little, *because* of it.

"About that joy you said we might find together..." Her voice was barely more than a whisper. "I want to look for it, Deke."

For one instant longer, his hand hovered. Then his fingertips stroked her cheek with an odd tentativeness, slipped down and back to the nape of her neck and drew her close against him.

Warmth flooded through every inch of Danielle's body, the pleasant warmth of a soft blanket folded closely around her. Peace, she thought. It was the last thing she'd have expected to feel while she stood in the circle of his arms. But it was understandable, really. With her decision made and the self-defeating battles over, she felt serene and tranquil. Perfectly at ease. Relaxed...

Then Deke kissed her, and the pleasant warmth became a scorching surge of heat. Tranquillity vanished; serenity turned to ash. Relaxation gave way to the desperate need to be closer to him, to be one with him.

He taught her about desire and showed her that what she had experienced before was merely a pale shadow of what she was capable of feeling. He taught her about passion, and together, very slowly, they explored all the secret corners of their hunger for each other.

And when she could stand no more, when her longing was too great to endure, he taught her about fulfillment, as well, and held her close afterward while she cried because it was all so beautiful. And then he kissed her tears away.

She lay in his arms, savoring the aftermath of love, and

knew that for the rest of her life she would be able to close
her eyes and relive this perfection.

No permanence, she reminded herself. No promises.

But there were also no regrets.

He was still asleep the next morning when Danielle crept
out of the apartment, but the square was already astir. She
took the indirect route, walking the couple of blocks to the
Merry Widow and telling herself that the fresh air would
make a good start to another long day.

But the glorious weather wasn't the only reason for walking. If she went straight from Deke's apartment to her car
at this hour of the morning, someone was bound to see.
But if she came back to the square later today—well, who
was to notice exactly how long it had been parked there?

And she just wasn't ready to face the speculation. Not
till she'd had a chance to savor for a little while in secret
the marvels that they'd shared.

She was setting the table in the dining room when Deke
came in. She knew it the instant he stepped into the house,
as though last night had created a magnetism that aligned
her nerves to his the moment he was within range.

She looked over her shoulder and smiled at him.

"Well, that appears promising," Deke murmured, and
moved closer. "I'll help in a minute. Just let me say hello
first."

His kiss sent a wave of desire through her, till her knees
felt as liquid as the pancake batter she'd just mixed.

When he let her go, Danielle laughed unsteadily at her
own incredible reaction and turned around to work again.
Deke started to nuzzle the back of her neck.

"I thought you were going to help," she said.

"I'm taking your mind off your work."

"You can say that again. Here." She pushed a handful
of plates at him, and he strolled around the table laying
them out. "Hey, you're not bad at that."

"I'll bet you could even get me a job busing tables at the Willows."

"Well, actually…" *Tell him about the sale*, her conscience warned. *Then he'll know that you intend to stand by the deal you made last night. And if you tell him now that you're leaving, the chickenhearted half of you won't be able to back out.*

"Deke," she said as she reached into a drawer for napkins, "we need to make some plans, because…"

He went as still as an ice sculpture.

As annoyed at herself for her clumsiness as she was at him, Danielle said tartly, "No, dammit, I haven't forgotten the rules. I wasn't suggesting we go shopping for orange blossoms, a house near a school or even a matching pair of recliners, for heaven's sake. I only meant that we're going to have to reach some decisions about the Merry Widow. It could be months before we even find out what we can do with it, and in the meantime—"

"Whatever you want," a sultry feminine voice said. "That's what you can do with it."

Danielle dropped the pile of napkins and spun around. "Kate!" *She's back*, she thought. *It's over*!

So why wasn't she happier about it?

In the arched doorway between the dining room and hall stood Kate Jablonski. Painfully thin and wearing far too much makeup, she was dressed in a brief halter top and the tightest pair of black leather pants Danielle had ever seen. Behind her were two men so tall and broad they made professional wrestlers look puny.

With an effort, Danielle tore her gaze away from the shorter but broader of the two—she'd never before seen a man with a rope tattooed around his neck—and looked at Kate.

"All I'm after is my furniture," Kate said. "You can have the rest."

Danielle's hand came to rest almost protectively on the polished walnut table. "But the furniture is—"

"Not that old stuff. Joe and I agreed I get everything in our apartment."

Where, Danielle figured, Mrs. DeCarlo was probably just now waking up. *I should call Pam so she can come over and see the fun*, she thought. "Is Joe here, too?"

"After the way he broke up my statues, if I never see that guy again it'll be too soon."

Danielle flicked a glance at Deke. "Told you so."

Kate waved a hand toward the men behind her. "Tad and Buck are going to move my stuff. We'll be out of your way in a jiff."

Danielle hoped Deke wasn't still so shocked he couldn't take a hint. "If I could get you to wait just a minute before you start, Kate…"

Deke said, "The guests aren't all up yet, so maybe you'd like to have a cup of coffee and talk about things."

Kate frowned. "What things? You aren't going to make trouble about this, are you? Do something weird like try to hold on to my furniture because this month's payment was late? This whole project was Joe's idea, you know. Talk to him about the money. All I want is my stuff, and I'm not leaving without it."

Danielle slid out the door just as Deke said smoothly, "Would you mind putting that in writing, Kate?"

Ten minutes, Danielle silently implored. If Deke could keep them there for just ten minutes…

Of course, a week wouldn't be enough notice to please Mrs. DeCarlo, she suspected. And if she had to wake the woman up to tell her that her bed was about to be removed from the house… This was not going to be pretty, she realized. Rubbing a hand across her forehead as she ran, she almost collided headlong with a guest at the foot of the stairs.

"Sorry," she said. "I'm very sorry. If I can just pass..."
She looked up to meet a glare so cold that she should have turned to ice on the spot.

At least I don't have to wake her up, Danielle reasoned philosophically. "I'm afraid we have a little problem, Mrs. DeCarlo."

"I'd say it wouldn't be the first. My bed was the most uncomfortable I've ever tried to sleep in. The bath is totally inadequate, and I dread the thought of what you'll consider an edible breakfast." She steamrollered past Danielle down the hall toward the dining room.

From directly behind her, the mouse cast an apologetic smile at Danielle.

"Perhaps in that case you won't mind so much that the room won't be available tonight," Danielle said sweetly. "The furniture is being removed this morning."

Mrs. DeCarlo stopped in the precise center of the hallway. "I have *never* encountered such an inadequate manager as you are, miss. Losing reservations and then making excuses about it. Putting guests in attics and garrets, then trying to evict them. You're even wearing the same clothes you had on last night. I should report you to the health department as unsanitary."

"I could hardly change when all my clothes were in a closet in the bedroom you were using." *So what if it wasn't quite the whole truth*, Danielle thought. It was close.

"And if you have the incredible gall to expect me to pay for the so-called service I've received here..."

Danielle had had enough. "Of course not. Your night's stay will be completely without charge. And since you have all day to make other arrangements, Mrs. DeCarlo, or to drive back to wherever you came from, please don't feel that you have to stay around and risk food poisoning by eating breakfast under my roof."

Mrs. DeCarlo opened her mouth, closed it, then opened it again. The mouse looked as if she'd like to applaud.

From the corner of her eye, Danielle could see movement in the dining room. Deke stepped out into the hallway and leaned against the arched door frame.

And he said, ''Well, this is a surprise. Danielle neglected to tell me you were here. Exactly when did you arrive, Mother?''

CHAPTER TEN

DANIELLE'S heart plummeted to her toes. Mrs. DeCarlo was Deke's *mother*?

And what did he mean, saying that Danielle had neglected to tell him the woman had arrived? How was she supposed to know? Mrs. DeCarlo had said nothing about having a son in Elmwood, and the names were certainly no clue. All he'd ever told her about his parents was that they'd divorced long ago; she supposed his mother might well have married again.

There were men who seemed attracted to the shrewish type, Danielle thought. Especially if there were other enticements—and in her case, there'd have to be. Property, or prestige, or money...

This is no time for me to be catty, she told herself.

Money. As a general rule, she paid little attention to the world of finance; when one had nothing to invest, the stock market didn't hold a great deal of fascination. But wasn't there a DeCarlo family that had something to do with high finance? Somewhere she'd heard about a DeCarlo fund, or bank, or brokerage firm, or management trust. Or maybe a stock...

In the back of Danielle's mind, a couple of random facts snapped together. A stock, that was it. She'd heard about it in an economics class years ago. The DeCarlo family held controlling interest in an odd, obscure little business that specialized not in manufacturing or service but in owning other businesses. A sort of quiet holding company whose stock had quietly climbed in value until it was astronomical—thousands of dollars a share. If Deke was associated with that family...

Deke. She'd always thought it an unusual name. Was it perhaps a nickname instead? A shortened form of a family name? Maybe Mrs. DeCarlo hadn't married again, just reassumed her maiden name.

And maybe, Danielle told herself, *you're letting your imagination run away with you.*

One fact remained, however. He'd told her so little about his family that she'd met his mother without even suspecting a connection. It was just one more piece of evidence—as if Danielle had needed another—that the spot she filled in his life was temporary. If he hadn't even told her his mother's *name...*

Last night, she had shared with him the most intimate secrets of body and soul, holding back only the one that she couldn't share—the fact of her love for him—because it would hurt them both too much if she said it out loud. But what had he shared with her? The joy of making love...and nothing else. Nothing that truly mattered to him.

The pain of facing that truth was like being caught in a cloud of wasps—not an inch of her escaped the sting. In her blind anguish, Danielle struck out at him. "*I* neglected to tell you she was here? I don't recall your saying anything about her coming! So don't blame me if I didn't rush right over with the news!"

The suspicion in his eyes had been there all along, but Danielle had registered it only semiconsciously, too caught up in her own shock to wonder why he was reacting that way. Now she knew; he thought she *had* rushed right over last night as soon as she'd realized it was his mother who'd arrived. There would have been time, after he left, for her to get into a conversation with Mrs. DeCarlo, to chat about what had brought her to town, to find out about her son.

He might even think that was why Danielle had changed

her mind about sleeping with him. Why, she didn't know. What possible advantage could she have gained?

But she knew she wasn't imagining the wariness in his face. She'd seen that look before—on the day Miss Fischer's will had been made public, right before he'd accused her of using her elderly friend to manipulate him into marrying her....

Well, this time, too, she'd done nothing wrong. She stood up a little straighter.

Mrs. DeCarlo seemed oblivious to the undercurrents. She marched across the hall to Deke and presented her cheek, and he obliged with what Danielle thought was no more than a dutiful kiss. With a wave, Mrs. DeCarlo summoned the mouse to her side.

Danielle, who had almost entirely forgotten the younger woman, looked her over with new interest. Perhaps the young woman wasn't a companion after all, but a much-put-upon daughter. There was no family resemblance, but then she couldn't see much between Deke and his mother, either.

"You remember Laura," Mrs. DeCarlo said flatly.

Not a sister, then, Danielle decided, or she wouldn't have to remind him.

"Of course." With no more enthusiasm than he'd displayed to his mother, Deke kissed the younger woman's forehead.

She smiled up at him, her face coming alive with a sudden brilliant beauty, and the light dawned for Danielle. *She's in love with him, and she's too innocent even to try to hide it. And Deke, being Deke, is doing everything he can to discourage her.*

"You don't deserve that she still takes an interest in you," Mrs. DeCarlo decreed. "And in fact, she's been seeing a wonderful young man—I had to tear her away to accompany me on this trip."

"And if you believe that," Danielle muttered under her breath, "there's a bridge for sale cheap in Brooklyn."

Mrs. DeCarlo glared at her. "I can't imagine why you're still here. Go about your business, girl."

For one instant, Danielle contemplated telling the woman precisely why she considered this little scene her business. But it wouldn't impress Mrs. DeCarlo, it wouldn't humiliate Deke, it wouldn't restore her own shredded pride, and it *would* embarrass the poor little mouse, whose only offense was to have fallen in love with a man who didn't care for her.

Been there, Danielle thought. *Done that. Maybe I should invite her to lunch so we can compare notes.*

At least it was clear to her now—not only what had actually happened, but why Deke thought she'd taken advantage of the knowledge, and of him.

His mother had arrived with her choice of a daughter-in-law, and Deke thought that Danielle, understanding what was in his mother's mind, had tried to short-circuit Mrs. DeCarlo's plans by drawing him back to Danielle herself instead. Even if to do so meant sleeping with him...

She could almost feel sympathy for him. The man who avoided commitment at all costs, caught between the two of them. Perhaps she should put him out of half his misery, Danielle mused, and assure him that he had nothing to worry about from her, that she'd consider herself lucky if she never had to see him again. On the other hand, he didn't deserve any relief—so she kept silent.

A creak from the staircase drew her attention; she looked over her shoulder to see the entire contingent of Merry Widow guests arranged on the steps, leaning over the railing, even hanging half off the landing to get the best view.

She turned to face them and made a theatrical bow. "Just a little extra entertainment, folks, free of charge. I'm sure you've heard about bed-and-breakfasts that offer murder mystery weekends? We're trying out the soap opera version. Breakfast will be served any minute now, as soon as Mr. Oliver figures out how to make pancakes. Because…'' She looked straight at him and said each word very distinctly, ''I am out of here.''

She was very proud of herself. She made it all the way to the square, to where she'd left her car, before she cried.

By the time Danielle arrived at the Willows for the lunch shift, she'd managed to cover up the traces of tears and pull herself together. She felt as if her smile was stapled in place, but the average customer wouldn't notice. And if she was lucky, the patrons who knew her best would choose another restaurant today.

Instead, the first people she seated were the Goodwins. It had been little more than a week since Mrs. Goodwin had broken the news that something was amiss at the Merry Widow. Danielle felt as if she'd aged five years in the meantime.

Mrs. Goodwin clucked over how tired Danielle looked, and her husband shook his head in concern. ''Told you it was a bad idea to make that place into a hotel,'' he said.

''I keep telling you, it's not a hotel, George,'' Mrs. Goodwin said, and Danielle left them amiably arguing about what should happen to the Merry Widow and went back to the maître d's stand.

Pam had arrived by this time and was transferring the contents of a fat bank bag into the cash register. She took a long look at Danielle and smiled slyly. ''Looks like you didn't get much more sleep than I did. So you and Deke are going to break the Merry Widow's curse after all, are you?''

''Actually, I'd say the real curse would be having to spend a lifetime with him,'' Danielle said crisply.

Pam's jaw dropped. ''But…I saw your car in the square

when I went home about three this morning…and I
thought—''

''That's why I'm so sure about the curse.'' Danielle
straightened an already perfectly arranged pile of menus.
''And that's why, as soon as I know when the Willows will
change hands, I'm going to Chicago and finding an apartment and getting my records up-to-date so I can start
classes at the earliest possible moment. Any further questions?''

Pam swallowed hard.

The dazed look on her friend's face made Danielle feel
like a complete jerk. ''I'm sorry.'' She put a hand on Pam's
shoulder. ''I'm furious and hurt, but that's no reason to take
it out on you. I owe you so much, Pam, for everything
you've done this week.''

''What are friends for?'' Pam frowned. ''As a matter of
fact, though, I do have one more question. What are you
going to do about the Merry Widow?''

Danielle shrugged. ''I can't see that it matters much.''

''Well, in that case… I've been thinking, and talking to
Greg. And if you're sure you don't want to keep it—''

''This morning, there's absolutely nothing in life I'm
more sure of.''

''Then we'd like to give it a try.''

''Be my guest.'' Danielle blinked. ''You mean… *What*
did you say?''

''Well, you know we've been looking at bigger houses
for months now.''

''The Merry Widow certainly fits that criteria,'' Danielle
said dryly. ''You've got three bedrooms now, right?''

''But if we take on a larger mortgage, I'll have to work
more, and we'll either pay a fortune in child care—if we
can find it at all—or leave the kids on their own far too
much.''

''Neither of which is a good option.''

"Building up my own business so it brings in that much money doesn't look possible, either—especially now that I'm losing one of my biggest clients. So I'd probably have to take a nine-to-five job."

"This doesn't sound like an improvement in the quality of life, Pam."

"Exactly—which is why we're still living in the cracker box. But if there was something I could do at home, a job that would let me be with my kids and still keep some of my accounting clients on the side—"

"Something like running a bed-and-breakfast?"

"Why not? The paying guests will take care of the extra expense of the bigger house, I'll still have most of my day free for my clients when the kids are in school and I can spend more time with them when they aren't. And don't feel you owe me for what I've done this week, Danny. I had an ulterior motive—I was trying it on for size, seeing if it just sounded like a good idea. But after the strawberry festival and all this tea-tent nonsense, it'll be dead easy just taking care of ten or fifteen people every day."

Danielle smiled. "Well—all right. When do you want to start? I mean, I'll have to talk to Deke before we can make it official, but…"

I'll have to talk to Deke.

There was a kind of resignation in the thought. Perhaps it would be just as well if they did clear the air. Get things straight between them.

They couldn't go on, that was sure. She'd believed she'd accepted the reality that though he was the center of her life, she could only exist on the fringes of his—but this morning had made it all too painfully clear that she'd still wanted more than he could give. Realizing how little of himself he'd shared, then seeing the suspicion in his eyes, had killed the magic they'd created the night before. No matter what happened with his mother, or Laura, or the Merry Widow, their affair was over.

And it was really stupid, she told herself, to wish that it could have lasted just a little longer.

She left a message at Deke's apartment, only half-expecting that he'd call back. No doubt he'd be busy for a while with his mother and the adoring Laura—too preoccupied, at least, to bother with Danielle.

But just an hour later, after Pam had gone and as the last of the lunch crowd was leaving, he came into the Willows. Even after her disillusionment, he could still take her breath away. *It isn't fair*, she thought. No man should be allowed to be so good-looking, so magnetic, so sexy—and so detached.

His gaze roved her face, and Danielle's skin warmed with the memory of how last night he'd made that same close inspection with his lips...how this morning he'd come into the dining room and turned her into quivering jelly with a simple kiss....

The last kiss, she reminded herself. If she'd known it was the last, she might have savored it even more.

You are truly a fool, she chided herself. "Thanks for stopping by, Deke. It wasn't necessary to rush if your mother and Laura are waiting for you."

He moved a little closer and rested an elbow on the maître d's stand. "However my mother made it appear, Danielle, there is absolutely nothing between Laura and me."

Danielle stared at him for one shocked instant before breaking into bitter laughter. "And you feel you needed to tell *me* that? Look, Deke, if you think I asked you over here to read you the riot act, you can relax. So we spent the night together—it was no big deal."

Sally came up to the cash register with a customer's check. Danielle rang up the bill and gave Sally her tip. She put the check in the bank bag Pam had left under the register and considered asking Deke to come back to the office or to a table in the now deserted solarium, where they could have a more private discussion. She cast a thoughtful sideways glance at him.

He was still leaning against the maître d's stand and looked, Danielle thought, a great deal more at ease than he had a couple of minutes ago.

Well, is anybody surprised? she asked herself dryly. She'd taken a load of pressure off him just now.

No, she decided, they didn't need a quiet corner or a private table; anything that needed to be said could be expressed right here by the cash register. This was a business discussion, so why treat it as a social event? Why draw out what was going to be painful for her? Why force herself to sit still and watch his reaction when she told him she was leaving?

"We were starting to talk this morning about what to do with the Merry Widow," she said. "And we will have to do something, no matter what happens with the Jablonskis."

"My attorney drew up an agreement this morning, and Kate signed it. She gave up all claim to the Merry Widow and everything associated with it. Then her two bruisers packed up all of her belongings and they went off to parts unknown."

"So if we can just find Joe and get him to sign…"

His voice was absolutely level. "We'll still be stuck with a bed-and-breakfast."

"Precisely." Danielle kept her tone just as steady. "And that's what I wanted to talk to you about. Pam's decided she wants to try her hand as an innkeeper. She's even getting Martha and company to take over at the tea tent so she can go to work on the Merry Widow again today."

She hadn't thought it was possible to shock him, but Deke's eyes had gone wide with surprise.

"We'll have to work out the details, of course," she went on. "Maybe we can make her the manager till we can get clear title, then arrange a sale when she's had time to get a business loan. My share will more than pay what I owe you for the roof, and then it'll be finished."

"And that's the way you want it."

It wasn't a question, and she knew better than to think he was actually offering a choice. "The sooner, the better. This way, no matter what happens, the Merry Widow will never rebound on us again—and that's worth nearly any sacrifice. I haven't particularly enjoyed this week."

"Not even last night?" The catch in his voice was almost a seduction in itself.

Danielle gritted her teeth against the unfairness of that question. "I found out what I wanted to know." She pushed the list of table bookings into place and looked straight at him. "I'll be here for a week or two, I suppose, finishing things up around the Willows before the new owner takes over. After that, Harry will have my address— as soon as I get settled, of course—so you can just mail me anything I need to see or sign. Since I won't be here, I'll trust your judgment about a fair price and all the details."

There was a long silence. She saw understanding settle into his face, but at the last moment her nerve gave way, and she turned her head rather than watch him show relief.

"Or have him mail it, if you'd rather," she said. She was amazed that her voice could stay so steady when inside every cell seemed to be playing hopscotch.

"And in the meantime?" Deke said quietly. "If you'll be here a while longer...it doesn't have to be over so soon."

Not, she reflected, *I don't want you to go*—or any of the

hundred variations a man might use if he actually wanted a woman to be part of his future. Deke's statement held in it the automatic assumption that there would be an end; the only question was precisely when it would come.

But of course she hadn't expected anything else.

"You made the rules, Deke. It's not my fault if you neglected to add one about how only you could call it quits." She shuffled a stack of scratch paper into a neater pile. "I'm sorry about offending your mother, by the way."

"Why? She's not in the least sorry about offending you."

Even in the midst of her pain, Danielle found a bit of humor in the comment. "In that case, I'll admit that I'm not very sorry." She held out a hand and forced herself to smile. "Well, here's to the end of a partnership. I'd say it's been fun, but—well, I'm sure you understand."

His fingers closed around hers, warm and tight. Almost as if he was trying to reassure her—and damn him for it, too, she fumed furiously. But she didn't pull away; to do so would have been showing discomfort, maybe even regret, and the last thing she wanted was for him to think she might be having second thoughts.

He kissed her fingertips and gave her hand back, then smiled at her and turned away.

And Danielle closed her eyes so she wouldn't have to watch as he left her for the last time.

She'd been away from campus too long, Danielle told herself. That had to be the reason she was having so much trouble concentrating in class and comprehending what she read at home. To make matters worse, by the time she'd gotten settled in her new apartment, the one summer course she'd been able to enroll in was far from being the most exciting she'd ever taken.

But she'd soon settle down to the routine once more. By

the time summer was over and the fall term began, she'd have readjusted to the pace of academic life.

And Elmwood and the Merry Widow and Deke would have faded away till she could pretend the whole episode had been only a dream.

She'd intended, after class was over, to stop in the library for another couple of hours of research. However, the clear beauty of the summer day drew her back across campus instead, toward home. She'd pick up her textbooks and spend the afternoon in the park, reading.

But the mail contained a thick envelope from Pam. Danielle's heart beat just a little faster, and she pushed the unopened letter into her backpack and turned once again toward the sunshine.

The park was only a block away, and at this time of day it was thinly populated—a few young mothers with toddlers and babies, a few older people sitting in the sun. And Danielle, who sat on a park bench away from the others and tore open the bulky envelope.

It hadn't been thick because of the letter, which was no more than a note obviously written in a tearing hurry. Danielle wasn't surprised—though she was a little disappointed—that Pam hadn't written more.

"What were you hoping for?" she asked herself. *"A minute-by-minute rundown on Deke's life, perhaps?"*

But the envelope contained a handful of pictures, and she pored over them one by one. The Merry Widow's kitchen, stripped to the support beams. A stack of new cabinets and appliances, enough to fill a whole bay of the carriage house, waiting to be installed. The attic suite, once more a single enormous room with the temporary walls the Jablonskis had installed ripped out...

That was odd, Danielle thought. Where were Pam and Greg going to live? Of course, what had been a barely adequate space for the Jablonskis could hardly house a couple with two children.

Not that it was any of Danielle's business, of course. She'd signed the sales contract almost a month ago now and sent it back to Deke. The papers had come to her by overnight express, without a note or a personal word attached—and she had sent them back the same way. Just a couple of bare signatures attached to a wordy legal document—that was all that would remain of the time they had shared.

She looked down at the snapshot of Pam's kids clowning on the front porch of the Merry Widow, under the new and bigger sign, and felt a telltale prickling against her eyelids. She put the pictures down on the bench beside her and fumbled for a tissue. The stack of snapshots slid on the angled seat, spreading out into an irregular fan of smiling faces and the evidence of hard work.

If anyone could break the Merry Widow's supposed curse, Danielle thought, and make it a happy home, it would be Pam. And she was glad Pam was to have the chance.

She blotted the tears from her eyes, but more took their place. They were silent tears, the kind she shed most often now, and she'd found the best way to deal with them was to indulge herself and get them over with. Trying to stifle them only made the next outburst worse. And though they came less frequently now, and were less predictable, she knew there would be yet another round to come.

When a shadow fell across her bench, Danielle was annoyed. The park was full of seats; why should somebody have to disturb her?

A hand reached down to stir the pool of photographs. A tanned hand, with long fingers and neatly trimmed nails… A hand she recognized. She looked up into Deke's unsmiling face.

"I see Pam's been filling you in on her plans," he said.

Danielle couldn't prevent a tinge of bitterness from creeping into her voice. "Any reason she shouldn't? I left Elmwood, not my friends."

He didn't seem to react. "Then she's told you the attic's going to be a honeymooners' paradise? A self-contained little suite, so a couple can retreat from the world for as long as they want and never have to come out at all."

"I'll bet you got a good laugh out of that one. So where are Pam and Greg going to live?"

"Over the carriage house. It needs some remodeling, but there's more square footage than they have now, and it'll be considerably more private than sharing the house with guests."

"And the kids can make all the noise they want." Danielle shook her head a little. "That must be some bank loan she got."

"Which reminds me." He reached into his breast pocket and pulled out a couple of folded papers.

Danielle couldn't help herself. "A fax wasn't good enough?"

"You can't fax checks." Deke's tone was perfectly even. "And I had to come to Chicago to do some business anyway."

"Of course." Otherwise, she thought, he'd have mailed this express, too. He certainly wouldn't have put himself to the bother of hand delivery. "Sorry to put you to the trouble of hunting me down. How'd you find me anyway?"

"Your downstairs neighbor told me you'd come this way."

Danielle glanced at the slip of paper he handed her, then stared. "This is more money than the sales contract said it would be, Deke. A lot more."

"The contract dealt only with the house. This includes

payment for the furniture and also for the goodwill of the business you were so careful to preserve."

"I thought I told you I'd trust you to be fair."

His eyebrows quirked. "You're not happy?"

"Fair to everybody—including Pam. What did you do, blackmail her into giving you this kind of money?"

"Blackmail Pam? With what? The shadiest thing she's ever done is..." He stopped suddenly.

Danielle shook her head. "No," she admitted, "I can't think of anything, either. But this is highway robbery, Deke. It's a wonder she's still speaking to me."

"You didn't turn your back on your friends, just on Elmwood," he reminded her. "And—of course—on me."

The sheer impudence of the statement took her aback. "Enjoying a little self-pity, are we, because you didn't get to be the one to say goodbye first? Have a good time, but I hope you won't mind if I don't stick around to watch." She stood up. "Thanks for delivering the check in person, Deke."

She'd taken just three steps when he said, "Now you can go back to making your conscience payments to the historical society."

She spun around to face him, too stunned even to try to hide it.

"Of course I knew," he said. "As soon as I took over investing Martha's little nest egg, I discovered it was a very interesting amount, coming in very interesting installments and over a very interesting period of time. Besides, you were awfully worried about what happened to that money—to say nothing of always being broke yourself—so it didn't take a lot of intuition to figure out that you'd been paying off a guilty conscience."

She was furious. "Yes, I felt guilty—because I always thought Miss Fischer intended the historical society to have the Merry Widow, or at least the proceeds from it. *Not* because I'd manipulated her into leaving it to me—because I didn't. But I don't suppose you'd believe that even if I could produce Miss Fischer herself to swear to it, so why bother to try to make you understand?'' She wheeled away from him.

"I believe you.''

Just three small words, said very softly—but they made Danielle's world hang suspended for what seemed to be forever.

"You're too innocent to have planned it, Danielle.''

She hesitated. "I suppose I'll take that as a compliment. Thanks for that much, at least. And for bringing the money. Now if you'll excuse me…''

She didn't know how he did it, but suddenly he was standing in her way, blocking the path. "Please,'' he said. "Will you sit down again, for a little while?''

Danielle wavered. Part of her wanted to run, but most of her wanted to do as he asked. Whatever he asked.

She sat down, almost primly, on the edge of the bench. Without looking at her, Deke took the seat beside her, far enough away that no accidental movement would bring them into contact. Careful, she thought. Always careful.

"Laura was the last straw,'' he said finally.

Danielle frowned.

"My mother was born manipulating people. You'd think after this many years she'd have learned some finesse—but with most people she doesn't seem to need it. She just pushes her way through. Her managing nearly drove my father crazy till he finally left rather than put up with it. Most of the time, I just ignored it. Heaven knew I'd had enough practice.''

She'd never heard such bitterness in his voice.

"From the time I was twenty-one, she's been parading women in front of me. Most of them were just like her—

scheming, plotting, maneuvering. Using any means at hand to gain the advantage.''

No wonder, Danielle realized, he'd assumed she was the same. ''But Laura wasn't like that?''

''No. Laura is much too sweet for her own good. She's malleable and gullible and not terribly bright, and her biggest wish in life is to please everyone around her. She doesn't deserve the hurt that my mother created by implying that if Laura played her cards right—Mother's cards, that is—I'd marry her.''

''You do care for her.''

''In some ways. Enough, at least, not to want her to be torn apart by my mother's machinations. But there was simply no talking to my mother. Believe me, I tried.''

Danielle sighed in half-willing sympathy. She'd tried to talk to Mrs. DeCarlo, too.

''That's when I decided to put as much distance between my mother and me as I reasonably could.''

''Elmwood?'' Danielle's voice dripped doubt. ''Of course. That makes it all perfectly clear.''

A brief smile tugged at the corner of Deke's mouth. ''Distance not only in the sense of sheer miles—I could have gone to Nepal and joined the Sherpas, I suppose—but in the differences in style and culture.''

''Oh, now that makes sense.''

''I was looking for a small place, just a bit out of the way, because I knew—I thought—that Mother wouldn't put herself to much bother to get here. And it did take her well over a year to give up on telephone nagging and appear in person.''

''Surprise,'' Danielle murmured.

''It was, too. I had no idea she was anywhere within six states. I don't think she'll come back any time soon, either,'' he mused. ''At any rate, that's why I came to Elmwood. I really did just about throw a dart at a map because it honestly doesn't matter where I live. I can keep track of the DeCarlo holding companies from anywhere—my father did it from Costa Rica the last few years of his life.'' A wry note crept into his voice. "I think it's because he could call out from there much more easily than my mother could dial in.''

Danielle, remembering the warmth and partnership and understanding between her own parents, shivered.

"But I was no sooner settled here than I met you...little Danielle, who was all the things I didn't know a woman could be.''

"And who still wasn't fascinating enough to make you commit yourself.'' She tried to keep the hurt from showing, but she knew when he turned to look at her that she hadn't been successful.

"No.'' The look in his eyes was almost commiserating, but his tone was cool, factual. "If it had gone on a little longer, I might have made that mistake. But...''

And I'm sitting here feeling sympathetic toward him? Danielle berated herself irritably. *What a waste of time to feel sorry for a jerk like this!*

"Thank you,'' she said tartly. "How flattering. But—luckily for you—Miss Fischer died right then, and everything blew up.''

If he agrees, she thought, *I'm going to kick him.*

"Suddenly, it seemed, you were just like those other women after all,'' he said. "In the nick of time, I saw the trap close—and I was damned grateful to escape. But you see, as soon as I got my breath back, I realized that I still missed you.''

"No doubt only because you hadn't gotten everything you wanted?'' Danielle asked sweetly.

"I tried to talk myself out of it. But every time I saw you, I wondered if you could possibly be what you'd seemed after all—because you were always taking care of

Harry, looking out for Martha, financing the damned museum. And then, out of the blue, it all started again. The Merry Widow was back like a bad penny—''

''And so was I.''

''Exactly. All of a sudden, you were gung ho to run the place—or rather, for *us* to run the place. You sounded so damned single-minded and innocent you couldn't possibly be real. It had to be a setup. I played along, waiting for you to show your hand. Eventually, I began to believe you didn't have a scheme in mind, that you really did think what you were doing was best for the Merry Widow.'' His voice dropped. ''And I found myself wanting you just as badly as I ever had before. Wanting you till I couldn't bear it. Till I couldn't think straight. Till, when you came to me, I didn't even wonder why that night was so important to me.''

That night was so important to me... Danielle felt a lump form in her throat. His admission wasn't much. But it was something—and from Deke, it was a treasure she could hold on to forever.

''It wasn't till I saw you face my mother down that I realized how terribly I had underestimated you. You really were what you seemed—straightforward and honest and precious and true.''

She closed her eyes and collected the words like pearls to string together into an heirloom necklace.

''But before I could tell you that—or even think it all through—you told me you were leaving. I thought I was just annoyed because I'd waited so long for you, and our time together would be so short.''

''You were annoyed,'' Danielle said bluntly, ''because you weren't the one doing the leaving. Because I wasn't cooperative enough to stick around till you got tired of me.''

''That's not very flattering,'' he admitted, ''but it's exactly right. It wasn't until after you were gone that I admitted the real reason I didn't want you to go—that you'd made a hole in my heart that nothing but you could fill. That it didn't make a damned bit of difference whether I wanted to make a commitment—it was already made before I even realized it. That the idea of *forever* wasn't so scary anymore—unless it didn't include you.''

Her heart was so full that she thought her ribs would break.

"Danny," he said softly, "I've had all the chances any man could ask for and I've messed up every one of them. I don't have a right in the world to ask for another. But I can't stop thinking that you couldn't have made love with me like that if I didn't matter at all to you. And if you can just find it in your heart to let me redeem myself…''

His voice trailed off. He propped his elbows on his knees and dropped his face into his hands.

"I think," she said quietly, "that I could bear to watch you try."

His head came up, and the hope and wonder in his eyes sent a rush of love through Danielle that put an end to any plan for further teasing. She held out a trembling hand, and he took it, laid the palm against his cheek for a long moment, then drew her near until she was nestled against him so closely that she was uncertain whether it was his heartbeat she was feeling or her own.

He kissed her almost clumsily, with an uncertainty that melted her faster than any amount of charming surety could have done, and then, as she responded, with a hunger that was almost desperation.

The tiny corner of her mind that had managed to hang on to rationality murmured, *This is Deke. You can do this— to Deke!* and the last tiny shard of doubt crumbled into dust. "Marry me?" he whispered, and all she could do was nod and pull him closer yet.

When finally the world stopped spinning around them and Danielle could begin to think again, she was conscious only of the warmth of his arms, the slowly steadying rhythm of his breathing, and contentment so rich and relaxing that she thought she might never move again. But eventually, reality intruded once more, reminding her that there were questions yet unanswered, decisions yet unmade.

"Deke," she said softly.

"Yes, darling?"

"It's not that I don't want to go back to Elmwood, but…"

He kissed her earlobe. "But you don't want to go back to Elmwood. It's all right. If you want to live in Paris…"

She shook her head. "Your mother might visit."

"After what I told her this time… Well, I of all people ought to know how difficult she is to discourage. All right, not Paris. If it's to be Nepal, I insist on a six-month trial, but anything else, I think I can handle."

"And I don't mean I never want to go back. But my degree is important to me. I've put it off so long." She swallowed hard. "And if you really can live anywhere…"

He drew back far enough to smile down into her eyes. "If that's all you want," he murmured, "I will cheerfully carry books, turn pages, quiz you for tests, bring you coffee, rub your aching neck…as long as you'll look up from your homework now and then and smile at me."

"I think I can manage that. Deke?"

"Yes, darling?"

"What shady thing did Pam do?" He looked puzzled, and Danielle went on, "When I asked if you'd blackmailed her, you started to say something—but I didn't realize till just now that you didn't mean you couldn't think of anything she'd done, but that actually there was something— and you didn't want to tell me what it was."

"Oh." He looked a bit sheepish. "She told me that you

were very unhappy, and when I mentioned that I was coming up here, she suggested I tell you that your father wants you to come home. It's not a lie, actually—I'm sure he'd love to see you. But Harry doesn't need you nearly as much as I do.''

She tipped her head to one side and simply looked at him, basking in the glow she saw in his eyes.

''I love you, Danielle. I never thought I'd say that to any woman. I didn't think there was a woman anywhere I'd trust enough to say it.''

She smiled, and whispered, ''I love you, Deke.'' And for a very long time, as he kissed her, she couldn't think at all. It was the rustle of paper, somewhere in the minute space between their bodies, that brought her once more back to reality, and she was startled to realize she was still clutching the check he'd brought her. It was crumpled now, and the heat of her hand had made the ink run on the signature. She looked at it, then up at him. ''Deke...would you mind awfully if I sign this over to the museum?''

His lips moved slowly along her cheekbone and grazed her temple. ''Of course I wouldn't mind. Unless you'd rather put it with the other half.''

''Your half?'' she asked dubiously. ''Where is it?''

''Are you always going to be suspicious of me where money's concerned?'' But his tone was nonchalant. ''I gave it back to Pam and Greg.''

Danielle pulled back from him and stared up into his eyes. ''After driving the hardest bargain this side of the Mississippi River, you just *gave it back*?''

''They're going to have a hard enough time making that business fly. A little extra capital can make all the difference.''

''You're the one who made it so difficult, Deke,'' she pointed out. ''You held them up as efficiently as a bank robber and then simply gave it back?''

"All right, I have to admit I pushed a little. I wanted to see just what Pam and Greg were willing to put into this deal—because if they were casual about it, they'd fail for sure. Better to find that out up front instead of when they reached the brink of bankruptcy. I have to admit they were pretty convincing, though. The things they're willing to do to own that place are nothing short of astounding. So—"

She shrieked with laughter and threw herself into his arms. "My hero," she gasped, and was tickled to see the faintest tinge of color rise in his face.

"Besides," he pointed out, "the museum got its cut last time around. Where did you think Martha got the idea she'd made a hundred percent interest in thirty days? As soon as I realized what you'd done—"

"You gave them yours, too?"

He nodded. "I told you my share was in a mutual fund— I just didn't say which name it was under. It just felt right, Danielle. We never should have owned that house."

"I'm not sorry we did."

He smiled down at her with a light in his eyes that made Danielle's heart turn over. "Me, neither," he whispered, and drew her close against his heart.

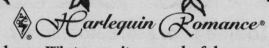

Harlequin Romance®

Rebecca Winters writes wonderful romances
that pack an emotional punch you'll never
forget. Brimful of brides, babies and
bachelors, her new trilogy is no exception.

Meet Annabelle, Gerard and Diana. Annabelle and
Gerard are private investigators, Diana, their
hardworking assistant. Each of them is about to face a
rather different assignment—falling in love!

L O V E
undercover

Their mission was marriage!

Books in this series are:

March 1999 #3545
UNDERCOVER FIANCÉE

April 1999 #3549
UNDERCOVER BACHELOR

MAY 1999 #3553
UNDERCOVER BABY

Available wherever Harlequin books are sold.

HARLEQUIN®
*M*akes any time special ™

Tough, rugged and irresistible...

THE AUSTRALIANS

Stories of romance Australian-style, guaranteed to fulfill that sense of adventure!

This March 1999 look for

Boots in the Bedroom!
by **Alison Kelly**

Parish Dunford lived in his cowboy boots—no one was going to change his independent, masculine ways. Gina, Parish's newest employee, had no intention of trying to do so—she preferred a soft bed to a sleeping bag on the prairie. Yet somehow she couldn't stop thinking of how those boots would look in her bedroom—with Parish still in them....

The Wonder from Down Under: where spirited women win the hearts of Australia's most independent men!

Available March 1999
at your favorite retail outlet.

HARLEQUIN®
Makes any time special ™

PHAUS9

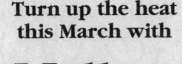

My Secret Admirer

Savor the magic of love
with three new romances
from top-selling authors
**Anne Stuart,
Vicki Lewis Thompson and
Marisa Carroll.**

My Secret Admirer is a unique collection
of three brand-new stories featuring passionate
secret admirers. Celebrate Valentine's Day with
these wonderfully romantic tales that are
ideally suited for this special time!

Available in February 1999 at your favorite retail outlet.

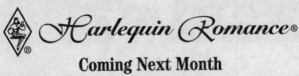

Coming Next Month

#3543 THE NINE-DOLLAR DADDY Day Leclaire
Ten-year-old Hutch Lonigan had walked into the Yellow Rose Matchmakers
Agency with all his savings and demanded the best man he could get for
nine dollars! The sleeping partner in the family business,
Ty Merrick, hadn't expected that man to be him. But one look at
Cassidy Lonigan, and Ty was hearing wedding bells. Only it was going to
take more than sweet talk and kisses to persuade young Hutch's stubborn
mother to walk up the aisle!

Texas Grooms Wanted!: *Only cowboys need apply!*

#3544 TEMPORARY ENGAGEMENT Jessica Hart
Bubbly Flora Mason had had plans to temp and travel. Her plans had *not*
included being engaged to her sexy boss, Matt Davenport. Only, Flora had
needed to save face, and Matt had needed a temporary fiancée. So what if
they were like chalk and cheese? It was only for two nights. But then, two
nights turned into three, then four....

Marrying the Boss: *From boardroom to bride and groom!*

Starting next month look out for a new trilogy by bestselling author
Rebecca Winters.

#3545 UNDERCOVER FIANCÉE Rebecca Winters
Annabelle Forrester has only ever loved one man—Rand Dumbarton. The
sexy tycoon had swept her off her feet, but their whirlwind engagement
had ended bitterly. She hadn't expected to have him walk back into her life
and hire her! Only it seemed Rand didn't want Annabelle to work for
him...he just wanted her!

Love Undercover: *Their mission was marriage!*

#3546 A DAD FOR DANIEL Janelle Denison
Tyler Whitmore had returned home after nine years to claim his half of the
family business. And Brianne was right to be nervous. When Tyler had left
he had taken more than her innocence—he had taken her dreams and
her heart. But unbeknownst to Tyler, he had given Brianne something in
return—her son, Daniel!

BACK TO THE RANCH: *Let Harlequin Romance® take you back to the
ranch and show you how the West is won...and wooed!*